Chasing Haggis

My Quest for the Legendary Haggis

ISBN:978-91-531-2834-2

Green Scene Publishing

Chasing Haggis

My Quest for the Legendary Haggis

Lachlan McGregor

Content

Dedication

To all those intrepid souls who chase the improbable, who embrace the unexpected, and who never, ever underestimate the power of a good dram of whisky to unlock the secrets of the universe. May your adventures be filled with laughter, questionable choices, and the occasional encounter with a surprisingly fluffy, albeit mythical, creature. And to my long-suffering kiwi flock – you're the best, even if you do prefer grubs to shortbread. This one's for you. (Especially you, Kevin, for that unforgettable farewell luau involving a slightly overripe mango and a questionable amount of fermented coconut milk.)

Preface

Let me preface this entire fantastical escapade by assuring you, dear reader, that I am, to the best of my knowledge, a perfectly sane zoologist. My methods may occasionally be unorthodox, my packing habits bordering on excessive, and my penchant for late-night pub quizzes legendary, but I assure you my sanity remains (mostly) intact. This book documents my journey to the Isle of Skye, Scotland, in pursuit of something utterly extraordinary – the legendary Haggis. Now, I understand that many of you may be scoffing right now, visualizing a rather unassuming, sausage-shaped creature. But I implore you, cast aside your preconceived notions. The Haggis I encountered were far from ordinary.

They were... well, I'll let the ensuing chapters reveal the astonishing truth. This isn't just a travelogue, it's a testament to the enduring power of myths, the resilience of the human (and haggish) spirit, and the sheer, unadulterated absurdity of chasing down a possibly mythical creature halfway across the globe. Prepare for a wild ride, filled with questionable choices, questionable cuisine, and a whole lot of unexpected hilarity. You have been warned (and possibly slightly intrigued).

Introduction

My name is Lachlan McGregor, and I'm a zoologist. Not just any zoologist, mind you. I'm a world-renowned zoologist (at least, according to my rather enthusiastic mother). My expertise lies primarily in the avian population of New Zealand – specifically, the charmingly grumpy kiwi. But my scientific curiosity, it seems, knows no bounds. That's why, when a cryptic letter arrived, hinting at the existence of a legendary creature known only as the Haggis, my tweed-clad backside was on the next flight to Scotland.

The letter promised a thrilling adventure, a test of my skills (scientific and otherwise), and a hefty sum of money – enough to finally upgrade my trusty, yet slightly moth-eaten, collection of field guides. What I wasn't prepared for was the sheer, overwhelming charm (and occasional stubbornness) of the Scottish people, the breathtaking beauty of the Highlands (even when covered in a light drizzle), and the utterly unexpected encounter that awaited me in the heart of the Scottish wilderness. This book details the highs, the lows (mostly involving questionable shortbread and even more questionable attempts at Gaelic), and the outright hilariously unexpected moments of my Haggis hunt. So, settle in, grab a cuppa (or a dram, if you're feeling bold), and prepare to embark on a journey that's as quirky, as unpredictable, and as delightfully daft as the Haggis themselves.

Chapter 1

From Kiwi to Kilts

Unexpected Assignment

Lachlan McGregor, a man whose tweed jackets outweighed his scientific publications (though he'd fiercely argue the point), adjusted his spectacles and peered at the missive. The envelope, thick and creamy, bore a postage stamp depicting a rather disgruntled-looking Nessie. The handwriting inside, however, was the real mystery: spidery, almost illegible, like a spider had dipped its eight legs into a pot of ink and then had a frankly terrible calligraphy lesson. It spoke of a legendary creature, a being shrouded in myth and mist, a creature so elusive, so enigmatic, that even the most seasoned cryptozoologist would balk at the challenge: the Haggis.

Now, Lachlan wasn't your average run-of-the-mill zoologist. He possessed a healthy dose of eccentricity, a penchant for questionable research methods (his "study" on the mating rituals of glow-worms involved a considerable quantity of luminous paint and a rather unfortunate incident with a garden gnome), and a collection of tweed jackets that could rival a small textile mill. But this? This was different. This was an adventure worthy of his most adventurous tweed jacket, the one with the strategically placed moth holes that he claimed added "character."

The letter, after much deciphering and the deployment of his trusty magnifying glass (a tool he used for everything from examining ancient manuscripts to assessing the ripeness of avocados), revealed an invitation. An invitation to Scotland. Specifically, to the Isle of Skye. To hunt for the Haggis.

Fuelled by a triple shot of espresso strong enough to melt glaciers, Lachlan embarked on his preparations. His meticulously packed suitcase, a triumph of over-preparation, resembled a small, mobile zoological laboratory. Within its depths lay not only his extensive collection of tweed jackets, but also: a high-powered set of binoculars capable of

spotting a single hair on a Highland cow from a mile away; a full set of forensic equipment for analysing potential Haggis droppings (a critical aspect, he insisted); enough batteries for his numerous gadgets to power a small city; a first edition of "Scottish Folklore for the Perplexed" (a surprisingly useful resource); and, of course, enough pairs of socks to last a small army through a particularly brutal winter. He'd packed for every conceivable contingency, including the possibility of encountering a clan of particularly aggressive midges and a sudden, unexpected outbreak of spontaneous bagpipe playing.

His farewell to his kiwi friends was a bittersweet affair. His closest companions, a colony of highly intelligent (or so he claimed) weta, seemed genuinely concerned by his impending departure. He'd promised them postcards, though he had serious doubts about the quality of internet access in the Scottish Highlands. The final farewell involved a rather tipsy gathering at his favourite pub, where he recounted his upcoming adventure with a healthy dose of embellishment and more than a few tall tales.

The flight itself was an adventure in its own right. He was seated next to a woman whose handbag held more haggis-scented perfume than a Scottish delicatessen, and the aroma, Lachlan later confessed, had nearly knocked him unconscious. The in-flight entertainment was a continuous loop of bagpipe music – a pleasant enough soundtrack, initially, until it played relentlessly for the entire twelve-hour flight, threatening to drive him to the brink of madness. At one point, he was certain a rogue bagpipe player had snuck onto the plane and was serenading the emergency exits. Theturbulence was intense enough to cause a near-catastrophic spill of his meticulously labelled collection of lichen samples, which resulted in a frantic cleaning effort involving an unexpectedly resourceful flight attendant and a rather impressive amount of hand sanitizer.

Finally, after what felt like an eternity of bagpipes and turbulence, Lachlan arrived in Skye. Stepping off the plane and onto Scottish soil, he felt the immediate shift in atmosphere. The air held a bracing, salty tang, and the landscape was nothing short of breathtaking. Dramatic cliffs plunged into the turbulent sea, misty glens shrouded ancient secrets, and the pervasive sound of bagpipes, though less intense than on the plane, hinted at the unique character of the island. His chosen lodging, a quaint (and slightly dilapidated) inn called the

"Whispering Heather," seemed appropriately atmospheric for his quest. Its proprietor, a wizened old woman with a mischievous glint in her eye, only added to the mystery. She informed him, with a knowing smile, that finding the Haggis was "no easy feat, laddie," and offered him a dram of something

suspiciously potent, possibly containing a large proportion of peat.

Lachlan's initial attempts to gather information about the Haggis were met with a wall of amused skepticism. The islanders, a charmingly stubborn bunch, weren't exactly eager to spill their secrets. His inquiries were met with cryptic riddles, sideways glances, and a remarkable number of "Aye, right" comments. One particularly memorable encounter involved Angus, whose beard appeared to be older than the standing stones themselves. Angus, after a long, thoughtful pause (during which he seemed to be communing with the very stones themselves), simply grunted and offered Lachlan a thimbleful of something suspiciously resembling peat. Another local, a woman with eyes that could pierce granite and a laugh that could shatter glass, simply told himto "look for the whispers on the wind," then proceeded to knit with unnerving speed and complete concentration.

Undeterred, Lachlan pressed on, his scientific mind already forming a complex algorithm to predict the Haggis's migratory patterns based on the consumption of local shortbread. He reasoned that if the Haggis had a particular fondness for shortbread crumbs, their trails could be traced. This plan was, of course, wildly optimistic and involved a significant amount of shortbread consumption on Lachlan's part, but he remained undeterred. His journey had only just begun, and the legendary Haggis, it seemed, was going to be far more elusive than he'd originally anticipated. The whispers on the wind, however, had piqued his interest. What secrets did they hold? Only time, and a significant amount of further investigation (and shortbread) would tell. The adventure was, as always with Lachlan, well and truly underway.

Farewell to the Antipodes

The scent of eucalyptus and damp earth clung to Lachlan as he stood on the veranda of his cottage, a small, tear-shaped island of sanity in a sea of rampant kiwi vines. His luggage, a chaotic mountain range of tweed and scientific paraphernalia, threatened to topple over the edge and bury the resident family of tuatara sunning themselves on the stone steps. Farewell, he thought, to the land of long white clouds, to the comforting drone of cicadas, to the surprisingly regular delivery of his favourite oatcakes. Farewell to the Antipodes.

His departure wasn't exactly a quiet affair. Mr. Fitzwilliam, the perpetually grumpy but secretly kind neighbour with a penchant for brewing illicit plum brandy, had insisted on a farewell "toast" that involved considerably more plum brandy than was strictly advisable before sunrise. Mrs. Higgins, the local authority on all things kiwi (both the bird and the fruit), presented him with a knitted Haggis – surprisingly lifelike, though perhaps slightly smaller than the legendary beast Lachlan sought. It was, she insisted, "for luck," though Lachlan suspected it was more of a deterrent against any overly enthusiastic Highland sheepdogs.

Packing, as one might expect from a man whose professional life consisted of documenting obscure avian species and whose personal life revolved around collecting rare tweed samples, was an epic undertaking. Besides the customary array of tweed jackets (in various shades of mossy green, heather grey, and surprisingly vibrant cerulean), his kit included a modified butterfly net (for gentle Haggis capture), a high-frequency sonic emitter (to locate Haggis through their alleged fondness for whistling tunes), a portableshortbread-analysis device (essential for tracking the creature's migratory patterns, of course), three pairs of binoculars (for long-range observation, close-up observation, and "just in case" observation), and an assortment of tranquilizer darts of varying strengths (because, as Lachlan reasoned, one could never be too cautious when dealing with a mythical creature of uncertain temperament). He also included a surprisingly large quantity of emergency oatcakes. One could never be too prepared for a lengthy, shortbread-fueled chase across the Scottish Highlands.

The actual farewell to his kiwi friends, however, was the most emotional. There was Kevin, the particularly opinionated kakapo who had developed a fondness for Lachlan's tweed jackets (presumably for their warmth and the lingering aroma of shortbread crumbs). Kevin, with a loud squawk that could curdle milk at fifty paces, bid Lachlan farewell with a distinctly grumpy peck on the cheek. Then there was Penelope, the cheeky weka who had a habit of stealing Lachlan's socks – a habit she continued right up until the moment he stepped into the waiting taxi, leaving him with an odd assortment of mismatched footwear. And finally, there was Horace, the grumpy but strangely loyal kea, who seemed to understand the gravity of the situation. He offered no farewells, only a knowing stare from his intelligent eyes, as if to say, "You're going to need more than tweed for this one, old boy."

Lachlan, slightly tipsy from Mr. Fitzwilliam's potent plum brandy and overwhelmed by the emotional weight of departure, felt a lump forming in his throat. He blinked back tears, which he swiftly attributed to the wind whipping in from the Tasman Sea. No, he told himself firmly, there would be no dramatic weeping. He was a renowned zoologist, a tweed aficionado, a master of shortbread analysis— not a blubbering mess saying goodbye to his feathered and scaled friends.

The taxi, a vintage model with questionable suspension and a persistent rattle in the engine, lumbered towards the airport. Lachlan, clutching Mrs. Higgins's knitted Haggis (which, he noticed, had developed a disconcertingly lifelike twitch in one of its tiny knitted legs), settled into his seat. He thought back to his home, the gentle rhythm of kiwi life, the comforting sounds of the bush. It was a life he loved, a life he'd miss, but the allure of the mysterious Haggis, the siren song of the Scottish Highlands, was simply too strong to resist.

The journey itself was an adventure in its own right. The airport was a whirlwind of bustling activity, a cacophony of rolling suitcases and announcements in multiple languages. Lachlan navigated the throngs of passengers with the practiced ease of a seasoned traveller, his tweed jacket somehow absorbing the chaotic energy of the terminal. The flight itself was surprisingly uneventful, save for a near-miss with a rogue sausage roll during the in-flight meal service, a minor inconvenience that Lachlan viewed with philosophical detachment. He spent much of the journey reviewing his notes on Haggis lore, meticulously cross-referencing accounts from obscure Scottish folklore with the latest research on highland fauna (which, admittedly, wasn't overly abundant).

As the plane began its descent, the landscape below transformed into a patchwork quilt of greens and browns. The undulating hills, the rugged coastline, the scattered villages – it was a breathtaking vista, a sight that filled Lachlan with a mixture of anticipation and trepidation. The legend of the Haggis, the whispers of its elusive nature, had drawn him to this remote corner of the world, a place where myth and reality seemed to blur at the edges.

He adjusted his spectacles, his eyes scanning the landscape for any sign of a fleeting glimpse of the legendary beast. He clutched the knitted Haggis more tightly, its strangely lifelike twitch now seeming more significant, more ominous, as if foretelling the adventures that lay ahead. The shortbread-analysis device lay nestled securely in his bag, ready for deployment. The butterfly net was at the ready. And most importantly, the various tweed jackets were strategically arranged for all possible weather conditions. Yes, he thought, he was ready. Ready for anything the Scottish Highlands could throw at him. Ready to face the elusive, possibly mythical, possibly shortbread-obsessed Haggis. His journey had brought him across continents, across oceans, and now, he was finally here. The pursuit had begun.

A Flight of Fancy and Turbulence

The air hostess, a woman whose smile could curdle milk at fifty paces, announced the in-flight movie: "Braveheart,"naturally. Lachlan, already nursing a headache induced by the aggressive perfume of his seatmate – a woman who apparently believed that liberally applying haggis-scented eau de toilette was a sign of refined taste – sighed. He'd envisioned a tranquil journey across the globe, a meditative flight filled with the gentle hum of the engines and the soothing murmur of the in-flight magazine. Instead, he was trapped in a pressurized tin can with a rogue bagpiper and a walking, talking haggis factory.

The bagpiper, a wiry Scotsman with a surprisingly vibrant kilt and a beard that could house a small family of badgers, had begun his performance approximately five minutes after takeoff. It wasn't a bad performance, mind you. The man could coax a surprising amount of melancholic beauty from the instrument, but five hours of uninterrupted bagpiping? Even Lachlan, a man who had once spent a week in the company of a particularly vocal troupe of kea parrots, found it a bit much. His attempts to discreetly plug his ears with his noise-canceling headphones were met with a glare from the haggis-perfume lady, who clearly considered the bagpiper's performance a sacred ritual.

"Ye cannae drown oot the glorious sounds o' Scotland, laddie!" she'd hissed, her voice like nails on a chalkboard marinated in haggis. Lachlan had simply muttered something about the joys of selective hearing and retreated further into his seat. The subsequent turbulence, however, was anything but selective.

The plane bucked and swayed, throwing passengers into a chaotic ballet of flailing limbs and spilled drinks. The bagpiper, thankfully, was momentarily silenced, his bagpipes tumbling to the floor in a tangle of leather and reeds. The haggis-perfume lady, however, seemed to thrive on chaos. She'd emerged from the turmoil clutching a miniature haggis-shaped stress ball, which she proceeded to

rhythmically squeeze while emitting a series of unsettling guttural noises. Lachlan, meanwhile, found himself engaged in an unexpected conversation with a rather portly gentleman in a tweed suit who claimed to be a champion competitive eater of haggis. The man, whose name was Angus (naturally), regaled Lachlan with tales of past haggis-eating contests, punctuated by loud burps that sounded suspiciously like bagpipes themselves. Angus insisted that the true appreciation of haggis lay not in its aroma, but in its texture– a claim Lachlan was not entirely convinced he wanted to verify.

The turbulence intensified. The flight attendants, normally unflappable paragons of airline efficiency, were now clinging to overhead compartments, their faces a mixture of terror and resignation. The bagpiper, having recovered his instrument, began to play a frantic jig that seemed to mirror the plane's erratic movements. Lachlan had a fleeting moment of existential dread. Was this how he would die? Crushed by a falling overhead bin, asphyxiated by haggis-scented perfume, or perhaps simply overwhelmed by the sheer awfulness of Scottish folk music played during a severe air pocket?

Amidst the chaos, a small, unassuming, brown paper bag caught Lachlan's eye. It lay abandoned near his feet; forgotten amidst the panic. Curiosity overriding his fear of potential haggis-related disaster, he picked it up. It was surprisingly heavy. He cautiously opened it. Inside was a neatly wrapped package of shortbread cookies. A tiny note was tucked inside: "To the brave soul enduring the flight from hell. May your journey to Skye be filled with more joy than this flight."

Lachlan smiled, a genuine smile this time, not a strained grimace masking terror. The shortbread, buttery and crumbly, tasted like a small, delicious rebellion against the chaos. Maybe this journey wouldn't be so bad after all. The rogue bagpiper, now playing a surprisingly upbeat strathspey, seemed a little less monstrous. Even the haggis perfume, while still pungent, seemed slightly less offensive when accompanied by the sweet taste of shortbread.

The turbulence eventually subsided, replaced by the calm hum of the engines. As the plane began its descent, Lachlan glanced out the window. Below, the Scottish Highlands stretched out like a vast, green tapestry, hinting at the adventures that awaited him. The flight had been a trial by fire – or perhaps a trial by bagpipes and haggis perfume –but he'd survived. And he had cookies. That was something.

The landing was a little bumpy, but surprisingly, the haggis-perfume lady was nowhere to be seen. Perhaps she'd been ejected from the plane during the turbulence, a fragrant human projectile launched across the

Atlantic. Lachlan couldn't help but harbour a small, guilty feeling of relief. He collected his luggage, navigating around a small, bewildered-looking sheep that had somehow wandered onto the tarmac (Scotland was proving to be a land of surprises).

As Lachlan stepped off the plane, the crisp Scottish air was a welcome change from the recycled air of the cabin. He took a deep breath, the scent of heather and peat a far cry from the scent of haggis. He looked up at the sky, a clear, brilliant blue. His adventure had officially begun. He already knew, with a certainty that defied logic and reason, that this journey would be far more bizarre, and potentially more fragrant, than he could have ever imagined. The legendary Haggis awaited, and if his experience on the plane was any indication, the path to finding it would be anything but ordinary. The thought, instead of filling him with apprehension, spurred a thrill of excitement through him. He had a feeling this would be a trip for the ages, a journey brimming with laughter, chaos, and perhaps just a hint of haggis. He grinned, adjusted his backpack, and set off into the Scottish Highlands, ready to conquer whatever surprises, fragrant or otherwise, awaited him. He even had a spare cookie for the road. One could never be too prepared for the unexpected in Scotland, especially when haggis was involved. And this was only the beginning of the grand adventure.

First Impressions of Skye

The taxi deposited Lachlan at the foot of a crumbling stone wall, the air thick with the scent of salt and something vaguely... sheepish. Skye hit him like a wave; a dramatic, breathtaking wave of rugged beauty and looming, mist-shrouded mountains. He blinked, momentarily disoriented by the sheer scale of it all. This wasn't the rolling green hills of the brochures; this was a land sculpted by giants, a canvas of brooding greys and vibrant greens, splashed with the wild, untamed energy of the sea.

His luggage, a rather battered collection of khaki bags and a suspiciously stained duffel containing what he assured himself was purely scientific equipment (mostly consisting of a collection of unusually shaped corks and a rather enthusiastically decorated butterfly net), felt ridiculously inadequate in the face of such majestic surroundings. He hefted his bags, the weight seeming to increase with every step he took towards the inn, "The Misty Isle," according to the rather faded sign leaning precariously against the wall.

The inn itself was... charmingly rustic. That's what Lachlan told himself, anyway. The truth was, it looked like it had been assembled from spare parts of older, even more dilapidated buildings. One window seemed to be winking at him with a decidedly crooked eye, while another was patched with what appeared to be a repurposed tarpaulin. The paint, if it had ever been paint, was peeling in generous flakes, revealing layers of faded hues that suggested a rich, if somewhat chaotic, history.

Inside, the air was a curious blend of peat smoke, damp wool, and something indefinably... Highland. A fire crackled merrily in a hearth that looked like it had witnessed centuries of storytelling, its stone face blackened with age and soot. A woman, whose smile lines suggested a lifetime spent battling the Scottish weather and even more lifetimes spent laughing at its capriciousness, emerged from a shadowed corner.

"You're Lachlan, aye?" she asked, her voice as rough and comforting as the granite cliffs outside.

Lachlan, somewhat overwhelmed by the immediate sensory overload, nodded dumbly.

"Aye, I'm Morag. Room's ready. Bit drafty, mind you. But the view's worth it. Especially at sunset. It's... well, it's Skye." She paused, as if searching for words to adequately describe something indescribable. "You'll be wanting tea. Strong, of course. And a wee dram to settle your nerves after that journey. I'd say you're looking a bit peaky."

Morag's assessment was accurate. The journey had not been kind. Between the haggis-scented passenger and the impromptu bagpipe recital in the aisle, Lachlan was ready for a strong cup of something hot and a long, uninterrupted sleep. But the anticipation of his quest, the allure of the elusive Haggis, kept him alert, his curiosity buzzing like a startled Highland bee.

He followed Morag down a corridor that seemed to shift and change with every step, as if the very walls were breathing with the ebb and flow of the sea nearby. The floorboards groaned underfoot, a chorus of creaks and sighs that spoke of countless footsteps and countless stories. His room, small but surprisingly clean (considering the overall ambiance), boasted a window overlooking the churning sea. The view, even in the overcast light, was breathtaking. Dramatic cliffs plunged into the ocean, their jagged edges disappearing into the swirling mist that clung to the mountaintops.

That night, after a hearty meal of something that resembled stew but tasted inexplicably like freedom, Lachlan sat by the fire, nursing a dram of whisky Morag insisted was "the nectar of the gods," and studying his map. It was a rather chaotic collection of scribbles, faded ink, and what appeared to be a hastily drawn picture of a rather portly haggis wearing a kilt. It had been given to him by a slightly eccentric antique dealer in Inverness, a man whose enthusiasm for obscure Highland lore was only surpassed by his love of haggis-flavored shortbread.

The fire crackled, casting dancing shadows on the walls, making the already quirky inn seem even more whimsical. The wind howled outside, a mournful cry that was both terrifying and strangely beautiful. He listened to the sounds of Skye – the rhythmic crash of waves, the lonely bleating of sheep, and, ever-present, the haunting melody of a distant bagpipe. It was a symphony of the wild, a soundtrack to his adventure.

The next day was spent exploring the immediate vicinity of the inn. Lachlan, armed with his trusty, if somewhat over-decorated, butterfly net and a notebook filled with more questions than answers, wandered among the dramatic cliffs and misty glens. The landscape was a constant source of wonder and confusion. He encountered sheep that seemed to regard him with an almost unsettling intelligence, birds that sang songs that sounded suspiciously like Gaelic curses, and wildflowers that seemed to shimmer with an inner light.

He also encountered a herd of rather grumpy-looking Highland cows. They stared at him with disdain, chewing their cud with a deliberate slowness that suggested they found his presence profoundly irritating. Lachlan, ever the polite zoologist, attempted to greet them with a friendly wave and a cheerful "Good morning!" His efforts were met with a collective snort and a simultaneous flick of their tails, a gesture that could be interpreted as either an insult or an invitation to leave immediately. He decided to opt for the former interpretation and moved on.

He spent hours lost in the labyrinthine paths that twisted and turned through the heather, the wind whipping around him, the mist swirling like a mischievous spirit. He felt utterly dwarfed by the landscape, yet exhilarated by its sheer wildness. This was a place where legends could be born, where the extraordinary seemed perfectly ordinary. And somewhere, nestled in the heart of this dramatic landscape, awaited the legendary Haggis. He smiled, a thrill of anticipation running through him. This was only the beginning. He had a feeling his adventure was about to get much, much stranger. Much more fragrant, too. He found himself hoping that the haggis-scented eau de toilette was an isolated incident. But then again, if he were to judge this trip by the standards of a normal holiday, the whole thing would have already been deemed a catastrophic failure. He adjusted his pack, pulled out another cookie, and continued his exploration. The search for the elusive haggis had officially entered a whole new level of quirky excitement. The journey, it seemed, had only just begun. And Skye, with its wild beauty and unpredictable charm, had already captured a piece of his heart. He knew, with a certainty that only a foolhardy zoologist pursuing a mythical creature could possess, that this trip would be one for the ages. The ages, possibly, smelling faintly of haggis. He chuckled, the sound swallowed by the vast, whispering landscape of Skye.

Meeting the Locals and their Skepticism

My first encounter with a Skye resident wasn't exactly a warm embrace. It involved a rather aggressive sheepdog, a woman who looked like she'd wrestled a badger and won (and possibly worn it as a hat), and a conversation that went something like this:

"Excuse me, madam," I began, attempting a charming Kiwi lilt, "I'm a zoologist from New Zealand, and I'm rather interested in... local fauna." I gestured vaguely towards the heather, hoping to avoid specifying the "haggis" part just yet.

The woman, whose face was as weathered as the surrounding rocks, squinted at me. Her gaze was so intense, I half-expected her eyes to spontaneously combust. "Fauna, ye say?" she replied, her voice a gravelly whisper that sounded like wind whistling through a rusty pipe. "Ye're lookin' for the wee beasties, are ye?"

"Well, yes," I stammered, feeling a sudden urge to blame my current predicament on the previous night's dram of something rather potent. "Specifically... the haggis."

The sheepdog, who'd been eyeing me with suspicion, let out a sharp bark, as if endorsing the woman's upcoming response. She chuckled, a sound not unlike rocks tumbling down a hillside. "The haggis, eh? And what might a New Zealand zoologist be wantin' wi' a haggis?"

This wasn't going as planned. My carefully crafted introductory speech, rehearsed numerous times on the plane, lay in tatters. I attempted a diplomatic approach. "I'm conducting research," I said, puffing out my chest. "A very important study on... unusual... culinary... mammals."

She raised a skeptical eyebrow, a feat I found surprisingly impressive considering the amount of wrinkles already residing on her face. "Culinary mammals, ye say? Och, lad, ye've come tae the wrong place for culinary anything. Unless ye fancy sheep's trotters stewed with peat smoke. Then, I might have something for ye." She grinned, revealing teeth that could probably crack a nut.

The sheepdog, emboldened by her approval, nipped at my heel. I yelped, momentarily distracted from my scientific mission. "Right, well, perhaps I should rephrase," I muttered, retreating a few steps. "I'm looking for information on the haggis, its habitat, its... social structures."

This seemed to pique her interest, though not in the way I'd hoped. A mischievous glint entered her eyes. "Social structures, ye say? Aye, well, they're notoriously secretive creatures. Like the fairies, only fluffier, and with a distinct aversion to parsley." She leaned closer, conspiratorially. "But if ye want to find them, you'll need to find the Whispering Stone."

The Whispering Stone? What on earth was that? Before I could ask, she winked, turned on her heel, and disappeared into the swirling mist, leaving me with a disgruntled sheepdog and a growing sense of bewilderment.

My next attempt at gathering information involved a pub – a delightfully smoky, dimly lit establishment called "The Wee Haggis". Ironically, there wasn't a single haggis in sight, only a selection of suspiciously strong ales and a clientele that seemed equally suspicious. I tried my "zoologist" line again, but it was met with roars of laughter, shouts of "another round for the Aussie!", and a bizarre rendition of a sea shanty about a particularly hairy sheep.

I attempted a more direct approach with the barman, a burly fellow with a beard that rivaled a particularly well-maintained badger sett. "Excuse me," I said, trying to sound authoritative, "I'm a researcher studying... the local wildlife." I emphasized "wildlife" this time, hoping to avoid the culinary mammal debate.

He stared at me for a long moment, his expression unreadable. Then, he slammed a pint down on the counter. "Wildlife, eh? Aye, well, we've got plenty of it. Midges that'll eat ye alive, sheep that'll steal yer boots, and tourists that ask daft questions. Think ye can handle that?"

He clearly wasn't impressed. He gave me the impression that my request for information on haggis was about as exciting as watching paint dry. And to think, I'd anticipated a welcoming committee, maybe some helpful locals, and most definitely not a pub that specializes in midges and existential dread. Instead, I was facing a wall of resistance thicker than a highland fog. It was clear the locals weren't just reluctant to reveal their secrets; they were actively thwarting any attempts to unearth them, treating me like a particularly bothersome gnat.

Undeterred (or perhaps stubbornly determined), I continued my quest. Each encounter was a masterclass in evasion. I spoke to a crofter who told me the haggis resided in a parallel dimension accessible only through the consumption of a specific brand of shortbread (I bought a box, ate it all, and experienced nothing but a sugar rush). Another claimed the haggis were actually mischievous spirits who could only be seen by those who'd lost a shoe whilst climbing a particularly precarious cliff (I lost a sock, but saw nothing but dizzying heights).

One particularly enthusiastic storyteller swore blind the haggis were guarding a legendary treasure, protected by a swarm of self-combusting midges. I'd have gladly traded a month's supply of anti-midge spray for a confirmed haggis sighting, but that didn't seem to be in the cards.

I started to wonder if the haggis were indeed mythical. Maybe this whole adventure was an elaborate prank, a Scottish version of a wild goose chase. Perhaps the haggis was just a spicy metaphor for the stubborn, enigmatic nature of the island itself. Yet the thought of turning back felt like defeat. I'd come too far, battled too many sheepdogs, and consumed too much shortbread to surrender.

The days blurred into a sequence of cryptic clues, frustrated attempts at conversation, and alarming encounters with exceptionally well-camouflaged sheep. Each night, I'd find myself back in "The Wee Haggis," drowning my sorrows —and occasionally my hopes – in potent ale, listening to increasingly elaborate tales of the elusive haggis. These tales, though often contradictory and wildly embellished, still held a flicker of possibility, a faint suggestion that somewhere, somehow, these furry little legends were real.

It became a game of patience, a test of endurance. Could I outlast the skepticism? Could I crack the code of silence that seemed to surround these mysterious creatures? The answer, I realised, didn't lie in the words of the locals, but perhaps in the very landscape that concealed them. I resolved to change my tactics. Instead of questioning the inhabitants of Skye, I would allow the island itself to guide my search. The clues weren't hidden in riddles and whispers, but in the wind, the mountains, the heather, and the whispers of the ancient stones. The journey wasn't just about finding the haggis; it was about becoming one with the mystery, one with the wild, untamed spirit of Skye. And so, with a renewed sense of purpose and a half-empty bottle of whisky, I set off once more, ready to let the land speak to me. I even managed to escape the aggressive sheepdog's attention, by strategically throwing a stray biscuit over a rather imposing fence. It certainly wasn't the kind of scientific methodology I'd usually adhere to, but it got the job done.

The next morning, I began my exploration anew, leaving behind the pubs and the frustrating conversations. My focus shifted to the landscape. I studied the terrain, looking for anomalies, unusual vegetation patterns, anything that hinted at a hidden life. This time, armed with maps, binoculars, and a far more cautious approach to overly friendly sheepdogs, I was determined to succeed. The search for the haggis was, after all, just a vehicle for a deeper exploration – a journey into the heart of a legendary land. The adventure was truly only beginning. The faint, familiar scent of haggis seemed to hang in the air, a beacon guiding me onward, into the heart of the enigma.

Chapter 2

Clues and Conundrums

Decoding the Riddle

The crumpled parchment felt like a roadmap to madness, more akin to a particularly cryptic crossword than a reliable guide. Lachlan McGregor, renowned zoologist and aficionado of all things tweed, held the ancient map aloft, its faded ink whispering secrets only partially revealed by the flickering candlelight of his rather dilapidated Skye inn. The air hung thick with the aroma of peat smoke and something vaguely resembling burnt shortbread – a fitting scent for an endeavor as bizarre as this.

The map, purportedly detailing the location of the elusive Haggis, was a masterpiece of obfuscation. Swirling lines resembled the frantic scribblings of a particularly caffeinated spider, interspersed with symbols that could have been anything from ancient runes to a particularly elaborate recipe for haggis itself. Lachlan, a man accustomed to deciphering the complexities of animal behavior, found himself utterly baffled. His trusty magnifying glass, usually his weapon of choice against the microscopic world, proved utterly useless against the cryptic symbols before him.

"Right then," he muttered, adjusting his spectacles, "let's see what we've got here. 'Follow the path of the whispering wind,' Hmm, evocative, but not exactly precise. And what in the name of Robert Burns is a 'cauldron of swirling stars' supposed to mean? Is it a celestial event, a particularly potent whisky, or an elaborate metaphor for a bog?"

He consulted his well-worn copy of "Scottish Folklore for the Perplexed," a book he'd initially scoffed at but was now clutching like a lifeline. It offered little in the way of concrete answers. The section on Haggis was disappointingly thin, mostly consisting of unsubstantiated legends and blurry sketches that could have depicted anything from a particularly fluffy sheep to a misplaced badger.

Frustration mounted, but Lachlan, ever the tenacious scientist, refused to be defeated. He pulled out his notebook, a meticulously organized tome filled with observations on everything from the mating rituals of the kakapo to the migratory patterns of the lesser spotted woodpecker. A new section, titled "Operation Haggis," was rapidly filling with frantic scribbles, wild theories, and the occasional expletive. He even attempted to apply his algorithmic prowess, famously used to predict the migration patterns of endangered penguins, to the task. His complex formula, involving variables such as the alignment of the stars, the average rainfall in Skye, and the local consumption of shortbread (a key ingredient, he hypothesized, in Haggis sustenance), yielded only a baffling jumble of numbers and symbols.

His initial attempts to decipher the map's riddles had involved a series of increasingly ludicrous experiments. He'd tried holding the map up to the setting sun, believing the light might reveal hidden messages. He'd even attempted to communicate with the map itself, whispering increasingly desperate pleas to reveal its secrets. The only response he'd received was a skeptical stare from the innkeeper, Mrs. MacTavish, a woman whose expression rarely deviated from one of permanent amusement and mild disapproval.

Days bled into nights as Lachlan tirelessly pursued the cryptic clues. The whispering wind, it turned out, was a rather literal phenomenon – a persistent gale that whipped around the rugged peaks of the Scottish Highlands, threatening to both blow him off a cliff and send his meticulously organized notes scattering into the heather. The'cauldron of swirling stars,' after much contemplation and several glasses of something resembling medicinal whisky, proved to be a particularly striking constellation visible only on the longest night of the year – a fact that was somewhat unhelpful given the current season.

One clue, however, did offer a glimmer of hope: a drawing of a distinctive rock formation, resembling a crouching sheep, perched atop a windswept peak. This, Lachlan reasoned, was a landmark that might actually be located. With renewed determination (and a significantly larger supply of shortbread), he set off on a perilous hike across the highlands.

The trek was arduous, a test of both physical and mental endurance. The landscape, while undeniably beautiful, was unforgiving. He slipped and slid on muddy paths, battled ferocious midges, and found himself frequently entangled in thorny bushes – a constant reminder of the folly of wearing tweed on a serious hike. His trusty compass, a gift from his grandfather, seemed determined to lead him in ever- decreasing circles, possibly out of sheer Scottish stubbornness.

Along the way, he encountered a variety of local wildlife, each encounter adding another layer of complexity to his already chaotic expedition. A herd of sheep, seemingly possessed by an unusual intelligence, regarded him with suspicion bordering on disdain. A family of grumpy badgers, decidedly unimpressed by his scientific theories, chased him up a tree. He even encountered a pair of remarkably philosophical squirrels, who, after a long discourse on the existential nature of nuts, offered him a single, slightly moldy hazelnut as a farewell gift.

His attempts to document these encounters, using his usual meticulous approach, yielded some amusing results. His notes on sheep behavior contained observations like "Sheep exhibit a disconcerting level of collective decision-making, possibly involving telepathy," while his badger encounter was summarized as "Badgers possess an unusual degree of hostility towards tweed-clad zoologists." His attempts to apply rigorous scientific methodology to the behavior of philosophical squirrels proved ultimately fruitless.

Despite the setbacks, Lachlan pressed onward, driven by a mixture of scientific curiosity and an almost desperate need to prove he wasn't completely mad. He was, after all, a world-renowned zoologist, and finding a mythical creature was precisely the kind of challenge he craved – or at least the kind of challenge that justified his rather extensive collection of tweed jackets. The thought of returning to New Zealand empty-handed, faced with the amused mockery of his colleagues, was enough to spur him onward, even if it meant enduring another encounter with the philosophical squirrels and their rather questionable hazelnut offerings.

Finally, after what felt like an eternity, he spotted it – the crouching sheep-shaped rock formation, perched proudly atop a windswept peak. It was a moment of triumph, a testament to his dogged determination and his almost supernatural ability to lose his way while simultaneously finding things. The rock formation, he soon discovered, was the key to the next stage of his quest. Carved into its side, almost imperceptible to the casual observer, was a series of symbols, significantly clearer and easier to decipher than the initial map. These symbols, it turned out, were not runes or a secret recipe for haggis, but rather a set of remarkably precise directions to a hidden valley, where, according to legend, the elusive Haggis made their home. Lachlan, having survived grumpy badgers, philosophical squirrels, and an alarming amount of mud, felt a surge of cautious optimism. The hunt, it seemed, was far from over.

A Highland Hike

The wind, a mischievous sprite with a penchant for icy fingers, whipped at Lachlan's tweed jacket as he began his ascent. The valley, nestled between two imposing peaks that resembled grumpy giants locked in a perpetual stare-down, was a breathtaking sight, even if it did look suspiciously like a giant's muddy bathtub. His sturdy walking boots, thankfully, were up to the challenge, though the same couldn't be said for his dignity, which had taken a significant battering courtesy of a particularly enthusiastic sheep who'd mistaken his backside for a particularly tempting bale of hay.

The path, or what passed for one, was a treacherous ribbon of mud and loose shale, weaving its way through a landscape that seemed determined to trip him up at every turn. Heather, purple and vibrant, clung tenaciously to the slopes, its delicate beauty a deceptive façade for its prickly nature. More than once, Lachlan found himself wrestling with thorny bushes that seemed intent on stealing his socks, a prospect he found utterly unacceptable. His trusty walking stick, a gnarled piece of oak he'd acquired from a rather taciturn old man in a village pub (who'd insisted it had once belonged to a mythical Scottish warrior), proved invaluable, acting as both a support and a surprisingly effective weapon against particularly aggressive thistles.

The air grew thinner with each upward step, the scent of peat smoke replaced by the crisp, clean smell of pine and damp earth. Occasionally, Lachlan would pause, his breath puffing out in white clouds, to admire the panorama unfolding

before him. Below, the valley stretched like a rumpled green carpet, dotted with the occasional sheep that looked remarkably unfazed by the dramatic scenery. In the distance, the sea shimmered, a vast expanse of grey-blue under a sky that shifted from brooding grey to fleeting glimpses of brilliant blue. It was a landscape both awe-inspiring and utterly unforgiving, a testament to the raw, untamed beauty of the Scottish Highlands.

Following the cryptic symbols carved into the rock, Lachlan navigated a series of rocky outcrops and narrow, boggy pathways. He learned to identify the subtle differences between various types of mud – the squelchy, yielding mud, the deceptively firm mud that would suddenly give way, and the particularly tenacious mud that clung to his boots with the desperation of a lovesick Highlander. He developed a system of mud-avoidance techniques involving a series of hops, skips, and sideways shuffles that would have impressed even the most seasoned Highland dancer.

Along the way, he encountered a variety of wildlife, most of which seemed equally bewildered by his presence. A family of red deer stared at him with an air of dignified disdain before gracefully bounding away. A lone heron, perched on a mossy rock, regarded him with an expression that suggested he'd seen far more ridiculous sights in his lifetime. A particularly plump field mouse, seemingly unperturbed by the giant lumbering towards it, even dared to nibble on a stray crumb from Lachlan's haggis sandwich (a rather daring move, considering the creature's notorious fondness for oatcakes).

The hike was not without its humorous interludes. One particularly memorable moment involved a close encounter with a grumpy badger who, upon discovering Lachlan's intrusion into his territory, unleashed a volley of surprisingly accurate mud projectiles. Lachlan, ever the resourceful scientist, countered with a strategic deployment of his now mud-caked haggis sandwich, a sacrifice that seemed to appease the beast's fury. The badger, apparently a connoisseur of fine Scottish cuisine, retreated, leaving Lachlan to contemplate the bizarre turn of events.

Another time, he was briefly held hostage by a flock of particularly assertive sheep who seemed determined to prevent his further progress. Their leader, a woolly behemoth with an expression of profound disapproval, formed a formidable barricade, bleating his displeasure at Lachlan's audacity to traverse their sacred grazing grounds. It took a carefully crafted offering of biscuits (a rather desperate, but ultimately successful, peace offering) to appease the fluffy dictators.

As the sun began its descent, casting long shadows across the landscape, Lachlan finally reached his destination – a hidden valley, shrouded in mist and mystery. A small, crystal-clear stream meandered through the heart of the valley, its waters reflecting the vibrant colours of the surrounding flora. The air hung heavy with the scent of wild thyme and something faintly...haggis-like.

His heart pounded with anticipation as he cautiously entered the valley. The silence was almost overwhelming, broken only by the gentle murmur of the stream and the rustle of unseen creatures in the undergrowth. The elusive haggis, the creatures of legend, were surely nearby. He was aware, that despite all his preparation, all his research and his rather soggy journey, his task was still far from over. The creatures were legendary for their elusiveness, and their ability to blend into their surroundings; if he wasn't careful, the creatures of legend could vanish as easily as the morning mist. He needed to proceed with caution, and he needed to be quiet.

He crept forward, his every step measured and deliberate, his senses alert. The light was fading, and the shadows were lengthening, making it even harder to spot the creatures. He squinted, his eyes scanning the undergrowth, hoping to catch a glimpse of the legendary haggis. His knowledge of the creatures told him they were mostly nocturnal; he had a better chance of spotting them now, as they began to stir from their daytime slumber.

A low hum, almost imperceptible at first, reached his ears. It was a sound that was both alien and strangely familiar, like the low rumble of distant thunder, mixed with the bleating of a sheep, and something else entirely that he could not quite place. The air grew thicker with the unmistakable scent of haggis – a potent blend of spices, herbs, and something indefinably earthy. He was close. Very close.

Suddenly, a pair of luminous eyes emerged from the shadows, reflecting the last rays of the setting sun. They were small, but intense, glowing with an otherworldly light.He held his breath, his heart pounding in his chest. Then, another pair of eyes appeared, and another, and another. From the shadows of the undergrowth, a family of haggis emerged, their forms slowly materializing from the twilight.

They were not quite what he'd expected. They were smaller than he imagined, and their fur, instead of the usual dark brown, was a vibrant shade of emerald green, speckled with silver. They moved with a surprising grace and agility, their short legs carrying them silently across the mossy ground.

Their eyes shimmered with an intelligent light, and their small snouts twitched inquisitively. They were like tiny, furry, emerald jewels. The sight of the haggis, unexpectedly vibrant and enchanting, was both astonishing and humbling. His journey, his trials, and the sheer amount of mud he had accumulated were all suddenly worth it. He had found them. The creatures of legend were real, and they were even more magical than he had dared to dream. He had conquered the mud, the grumpy badgers, the philosophical squirrels, the sheep-dictators and the near-impossible map. He had, against all odds, reached the land of legend. And what awaited him was even more unexpected than he could have possibly have imagined.

Close Encounters of the Woolly Kind

The air vibrated with the buzz of unseen insects, a counterpoint to the rhythmic bleating of sheep that echoed from the valley below. Lachlan, his tweed jacket now adorned with a rather impressive collection of burrs and mud splatters, cautiously approached a cluster of rocks. He'd been following a trail of what he could only describe as"remarkably oversized, brightly coloured rabbit droppings,"a clue significantly more bizarre than anything he'd encountered in his years studying New Zealand wildlife.

From behind the rocks emerged, not a giant rabbit, but a family of Highland cows, their shaggy coats the colour of burnt caramel. They regarded him with an unnerving calm, their large, dark eyes seeming to assess his suitability as a potential scratching post. Lachlan, recalling a particularly unpleasant encounter with a similar bovine family in County Clare, opted for a slow, deliberate retreat. His scientific curiosity, however, outweighed his fear. He pulled out his notebook, scribbling furiously: "Bos taurus, Highland breed. Appears to possess an abnormally high tolerance for human proximity. Further research required. Avoid direct eye contact. Do not offer biscuits." He added a postscript: "Biscuits may cause aggressive mooing."

His next encounter was significantly less placid. A grumpy badger, seemingly the overlord of this particular patch of heather, launched a verbal assault that would have made a seasoned sailor blush. It involved a surprisingly wide vocabulary of growls, snorts, and guttural rumbles, all delivered with the conviction of a seasoned barrister presenting a particularly damning case. Lachlan, ever the diplomat, responded with a series of gentle hand gestures and a rather unconvincing whistling rendition of "Amazing Grace." The badger, unimpressed, responded by attempting to uproot a particularly stubborn clump of heather, presumably to hurl at the offending zoologist. Lachlan retreated swiftly, muttering something about the aggressive territorial behaviour of the Meles meles species. His scientific observation concluded with, "Further research strongly discouraged. Avoid interaction. Carry large stick (preferably with pointy end)."

Further up the slope, a flurry of activity near a small stream caught his attention. A pair of otters, sleek and playful, were engaged in a surprisingly sophisticated game of water polo, using pebbles as the ball. Their athleticism was breathtaking, their teamwork impeccable. Lachlan, captivated, forgot his scientific detachment and simply watched, mesmerized. His notebook remained untouched, his pen unused. The otters, seemingly sensing his admiration, paused their game and regarded him with curious, intelligent eyes. One of them even tossed him a particularly smooth, well-worn pebble, a gesture of peace, or perhaps a challenge to join their aquatic game. Lachlan declined politely, respecting their space and realising that not every encounter needed a detailed scientific analysis. He scribbled in his notebook, "Lutra lutra. Remarkably playful and intelligent. Observation suggests a complex social structure involving highly coordinated aquatic sports. Further research recommended, involving possibly waterproof attire."

His attempt to decipher the next clue – a series

of peculiar markings on a rock face – proved more challenging. He'd determined it was some form of ancient Pictish symbol, but his knowledge of Pictish script was limited to what he'd gleaned from a rather unreliable travel guide. He spent a good hour squinting at the symbols, muttering to himself, occasionally consulting his well-worn copy of "A Beginner's Guide to Deciphering Pictish Runes (For the Utterly Confused)." He concluded the glyphs depicted a rather detailed recipe for Haggis, but with an alarming number of unidentifiable ingredients (including what looked

suspiciously like crushed unicorn horn and the dried tears of a weeping willow). His only real conclusion was to seek some local expert advice.

As twilight settled, casting long, dramatic shadows across the valley, Lachlan's attention was diverted by a symphony of rustling in the bushes. This time, however, it wasn't a badger, but a flock of sheep, seemingly led by a particularly formidable ewe, who appeared to be staging a full-scale rebellion against a rather unfortunate shepherd who was trying to herd them towards a rather dilapidated looking shed. The ewe, with the determination of a seasoned general, organized her flock into a perfectly executed tactical retreat, using strategic positions such as rocky outcrops and surprisingly well-placed clumps of heather to avoid the shepherd's every attempt to capture them. Lachlan, captivated by the display of ovine military prowess, forgot all about the mysterious runes and the Haggis recipe. He noted down, "Ovis aries, Highland breed. Exhibit extraordinary tactical skills and a remarkable level of coordinated defense. Shepherds advised to rethink herding strategy. Further research suggested, possibly involving camouflage attire."

As the stars began to prick the darkening sky, Lachlan finally reached a small, secluded glen. The air hung heavy with the scent of heather and damp earth. Exhausted but exhilarated, he collapsed onto a mossy rock, the events of the day swirling around him like a kaleidoscope of furry, feathered, and occasionally grumpy creatures. He had encountered a menagerie of Highland wildlife, each interaction adding another piece to his ever more complex understanding of this magical land. He had failed to decipher the Pictish runes, but he had gained a profound appreciation for the cunning of Highland sheep and the extraordinary athleticism of otters. His scientific notes were a delightful mix of accurate observations and wildly imaginative interpretations, a testament to his somewhat unconventional approach to zoological research. As he drifted off to sleep, under a blanket of stars, he could almost hear the faint bleating of sheep and the distant rumble of a disgruntled badger, a soothing lullaby in the heart of the Scottish Highlands. Tomorrow, he would seek out the elusive Haggis, armed with his newfound knowledge and a healthy dose of skepticism, and with his trusty notebook filled with more than just scientific data but a colourful tapestry of his encounters in the Highlands. The search continued.

The Pub Quiz Caper

The aroma of peat smoke and something vaguely resembling deep-fried haggis hung heavy in the air of the "Wee Dram," a pub whose name, Lachlan noted with amusement, was remarkably accurate. He'd arrived, mud-caked and slightly dishevelled, hoping a pint of something robust would restore his flagging spirits and perhaps offer a clue in his quest. The pub quiz, it turned out, was precisely the kind of unexpected opportunity he needed.

Agnes, the quiz hostess, had a commanding presence with her formidable raven locks and surprisingly delicate tone. She cast a piercing glance around the room, capable of souring milk, before proclaiming, "Alright folks! First question: During the twilight hours, what is the predominant hue of a Highland cow's udder?""

Lachlan, armed with his notebook filled with significantly less useful information, exchanged a nervous glance with the only other participant who seemed as bewildered as he was—a wizened old man named Hamish, who wore a kilt that appeared older than the pub itself. Hamish, it turned out, possessed a wealth of local lore, a sharp wit, and a disturbingly accurate knowledge of the precise shade of twilight udder. He offered a knowing wink and a mumbled, "Think, laddie, think!"

The quiz progressed through a series of questions that veered wildly from the mundane ("What is the capital of Scotland?") to the utterly bizarre ("If a banshee were to knit you a jumper, what yarn would she use?"). Lachlan's scientific training served him surprisingly poorly; he knew the life cycle of the New Zealand kakapo but had no idea what a "wee beastie" was, let alone its preferred nesting habitat. Hamish, however, was a font of seemingly endless knowledge, his answers punctuated by grunts of satisfaction and the occasional dramatic sigh.

Agnes, the quizmaster, observed their alliance with a lighthearted disconnection. "You two make quite the duo," she laughed, her locks swaying gently. "One is immersed in science while the other is... well, entranced by magic, I suppose."

During a particularly challenging round – involving a surprisingly complex riddle about the mating rituals of Highland stags and the precise location of a particularly elusive clump of heather – Hamish leaned in conspiratorially. "This one," he whispered, his voice raspy, "requires knowledge only passed down through generations. The secret to finding the Haggis, my friend, lies not in science, but in storytelling."

Hamish revealed that the Haggis weren't merely creatures of myth; they were intensely shy, sensitive beings who thrived on being entirely undisturbed. He described them not as furry beasts, but as shimmering entities, almost invisible to the casual observer, and their presence often revealed by subtle shifts in the natural world – a sudden bloom of wildflowers in an unlikely spot, a peculiar shimmer in the air.

The next question threw them a curveball: "Describe the sound a Haggis makes when it's happy."

Lachlan, convinced he was hallucinating, stared blankly. Hamish, however, was ready. He closed his eyes, inhaled deeply, and let out a sound that can only be described as a cross between a contented sigh, a soft whistle, and the distant rumble of a particularly jovial thunderstorm. The quizmaster nodded approvingly. "Aye," she declared, "that'll do."

Their unlikely alliance forged, Lachlan and Hamish left the pub under a sky dusted with stars. The night air hummed with the energy of the Highlands, a palpable sense of mystery hanging in the air. Hamish pointed toward a distant ridge, silhouetted against the night sky.

"The Old Woman of Storr," he announced, gesturing to a dramatic rock formation. "There's a tale... a story... connected to the Haggis. Legend says they appear only to those who truly listen."

The climb was treacherous, the path barely

visible under the blanket of darkness. Lachlan, fuelled by a mixture of curiosity, several pints of ale, and the unwavering optimism of a seasoned zoologist, followed Hamish without complaint. Hamish, meanwhile, seemed to navigate the terrain with supernatural ease. He stumbled over loose rocks, but never fell.

As dawn broke, painting the sky in hues of pink and orange, they reached a hidden plateau overlooking the sea. The Old Woman of Storr loomed before them, its jagged silhouette etched against the morning mist. Hamish stopped, then pointed.

"Listen," he whispered.

Lachlan strained his ears. He initially heard only the wind whistling through the rocks and the distant cry of a seabird. Then he heard it. A faint humming, almost imperceptible, yet undeniably there. A soft, pulsating melody, like a heartbeat of the land itself. He felt a peculiar tingling sensation, a sense of unseen energy that enveloped him. As the sunlight pierced the mist, a group of small, fluffy creatures appeared in the heather. They were unlike anything he'd ever seen.

They were iridescent, their fur shimmering with an otherworldly glow. They weren't the shaggy, sausage-shaped beasts of folklore. These were delicate, ethereal creatures, their eyes twinkling with an ancient wisdom. They were, undeniably, Haggis. Not exactly the scientific specimens he expected, but certainly unforgettable.

As the sun rose higher, painting the heather in a golden light, the Haggis began to move, their tiny hooves barely

disturbing the dew-kissed grass. Hamish smiled serenely, his eyes twinkling with a knowing glint. "They only appear to those who are open to hearing their stories," he murmured, his voice as soft as the early morning breeze.

Lachlan, utterly speechless, watched them disappear into the heather, leaving behind only the lingering hum in the air and a profound understanding that sometimes, the most extraordinary discoveries are found not in scientific data, but in the heart of a good story, shared in a dimly lit pub, and followed by a surprisingly arduous hike. His scientific notes remained largely unchanged – the observations remained firmly rooted in reality, but now, a new chapter had been added, one that blended hard scientific data with a generous dose of legend, folklore and pure, unadulterated wonder. The Pub Quiz Caper, it was officially christened in his notes, a footnote in his increasingly colourful and utterly captivating quest for the Haggis.

The Shepherds Secret

The next morning dawned crisp and clear, the

Scottish Highlands bathed in a golden light that seemed to amplify the already dramatic landscape. Lachlan, fuelled by a surprisingly hearty Scottish breakfast of porridge, black pudding (a culinary experience he was still processing), and several cups of strong tea, felt a renewed sense of purpose. The pub quiz had yielded nothing concrete in terms of Haggis sightings, but it had planted a seed – a rumour, whispered amongst the locals, about an old shepherd who knew things, things nobody else dared to speak of.

This shepherd, a wizened old fellow named Hamish MacTavish, lived in a croft perched precariously on a windswept hillside, his only companion a sheepdog named Angus, whose stare could curdle milk. Finding Hamish's croft proved to be a minor adventure in itself. The aged shepherd, going by the name of Hamish MacTavish, resided in a precarious croft situated atop a windswept hillside, with only his loyal sheepdog Angus for company, whose intense gaze had the power to curdle milk. Locating Hamish's croft proved to be a mini adventure in itself. Lachlan's Land Rover, suitable for the rugged terrain of Skye, groaned and grumbled with every jolt, threatening to shed its various components at any given moment. Eventually, he abandoned the vehicle a good mile away from the croft and trekked the rest of the way on foot, his tweed jacket getting increasingly snagged on prickly shrubs.

Hamish's croft was a charming ruin, a testament to the resilience of both man and stone. Smoke curled lazily from a chimney, hinting at a peat fire within, and a scattering of sheep grazed peacefully nearby, seemingly oblivious to the wind's persistent attempts to sweep them off the hillside. Angus, the sheepdog, greeted Lachlan with a low growl, his eyes unwavering, assessing the zoologist with the suspicion only a canine guardian can muster.

Hamish himself emerged from the croft, a figure as weathered and rugged as the landscape surrounding him. He was tall and lean, his face a roadmap of wrinkles etched by years spent battling the elements. His eyes, however, held a spark of intelligence that belied his age. He was clad in a thick, hand-knitted sweater, the colour of peat, and trousers patched in a multitude of places.His hand cradled a knotted staff, evidence of the endless journeys he had taken through these hills.

"You're the one from the Wee Dram, aye?" he rasped, his voice as gravelly as the stones beneath Lachlan's boots.

Lachlan, slightly intimidated but determined, nodded. "Yes, Mr. MacTavish. I understand you know... things." He paused, searching for the right words. "Things about the Haggis."

Hamish chuckled, a dry, crackling sound like autumn leaves underfoot. "The Haggis. Aye, I've heard whispers. Tales spun in the dark, over glasses of something stronger than tea."

He paused, staring intensely at Lachlan, his eyes searching his very soul. "Why do you seek them, this... elusive creature?"

Lachlan explained his quest, his scientific curiosity, his fascination with the legend. He spoke of his journey, his encounters with the islanders, and the cryptic clues that had led him to Hamish's door. He laid out his reasoning, a blend of scientific observation and folklore, meticulously documented in his notebook, complete with drawings of questionable artistic merit.

Hamish listened patiently, his gaze never wavering. When Lachlan finished, a long silence descended, broken only by the bleating of sheep and the whistling wind. Finally, Hamish spoke, his voice low and conspiratorial. "The Haggis," he began, leaning closer, "they aren't what you think they are."

Lachlan's eyebrows shot up. "What do you mean?"

Hamish tapped his walking stick against the rough stone floor. "They aren't just... animals. They're guardians. Guardians of something far older than these hills, something... magical."

He then proceeded to reveal a cryptic riddle, delivered in a thick Scottish brogue that required Lachlan to ask for several repetitions and clarifications. The riddle spoke of a "stone that sings," a "stream that sleeps," and a "wind that whispers secrets." Each phrase seemed to evoke a specific location on the island, locations Lachlan recognized from his map.

"The stone that sings... that's likely the standing stones at Dunvegan," Lachlan mused aloud, consulting his well-worn map. "And the stream that sleeps... could that be the Allt Dearg? It's known for its quiet, almost still waters." The wind that whispers secrets was more challenging, a more generalized concept.

Hamish nodded slowly. "The wind... it speaks to those who listen. It will guide you. But be warned, the path is not easy. Only those with a pure heart and a keen ear will find what they seek." He handed Lachlan a small, smooth stone, cool to the touch. "Take this. It will help you hear the wind's song."

The stone felt strangely warm in Lachlan's hand, radiating a subtle energy. He thanked Hamish profusely, his mind racing. The clues were far more metaphorical than he'd anticipated. This wasn't a simple case of tracking an elusive animal; this was a riddle wrapped in a mystery, shrouded in the very heart of the Scottish Highlands.

As Lachlan began his descent from the croft, Angus, the sheepdog, surprisingly trotted alongside him, a silent, watchful companion. The sun was beginning to dip below the horizon, casting long shadows across the landscape.

Lachlan felt a thrill course through him, a

mixture of excitement and trepidation. He was closer than ever, he felt it in his bones. The Haggis, it seemed, weren't just an animal; they were keepers of secrets, guardians of a mystical energy embedded deep within the very soul of Skye.

His journey, far from over, had just entered its most challenging and intriguing phase. The "stone that sings" beckoned, its location echoing in his mind, promising a revelation that would rewrite everything he thought he knew about the Haggis, about Skye, and perhaps about the nature of reality itself. Armed with Hamish's cryptic clues, Lachlan's scientific precision was now interwoven with a touch of folklore and a generous helping of fantastical possibility. The quest for the Haggis had taken an unexpected turn, leading him down a path as winding and mysterious as the very Highlands themselves.

The next few days were spent meticulously following Hamish's clues. The standing stones at Dunvegan hummed with an almost imperceptible energy when he touched them, a faint vibration resonating through his fingers. The Allt Dearg, the "stream that sleeps", flowed with an unnatural stillness, its surface mirroring the sky with an unsettling clarity. And the wind, ah, the wind! It was as if the very air itself whispered secrets, carrying hints and whispers on its currents. Sometimes, in the quieter moments, he could almost hear the rhythm of a hidden pulse, a heartbeat resonating from the heart of the island.

Lachlan found himself spending hours perched on windswept hillsides, listening intently, trying to decipher the whispers of the wind, seeking a pattern, a clue. He felt utterly ridiculous at times, engaging in what he was sure would be considered by his more empirically minded colleagues as unscientific behaviour. Yet, there was a strange pull, an undeniable lure leading him onwards. He sketched furiously in his notebook, documenting the landscape, the wind patterns, the almost imperceptible shifts in the energy around him. His scientific notes were becoming intertwined with mystical interpretations, a curious blend of fact and fantasy.

One evening, perched atop a hill overlooking the sea, a sudden gust of wind tore past him, carrying a peculiar scent– the unmistakable aroma of peat smoke and, yes, deep-fried haggis. Following the scent, aided by the intuitive guidance of Angus, the sheepdog, who seemed to know exactly where they were headed, he stumbled upon a hidden valley, concealed within the heart of the highlands. There, beneath the watchful gaze of the ancient stones, nestled amongst the heather, was a family of Haggis.

They were unlike anything Lachlan had ever imagined. They were, in fact, not fluffy, sausage-shaped creatures at all but rather a small herd of shaggy, deer-like creatures, with coats the colour of heather and eyes that shimmered with an uncanny intelligence. They were smaller than he anticipated, but held an almost magical quality. They were watching him, observing his approach with curious, intelligent eyes.

His scientific training kicked in. He started taking detailed notes, sketching their unique physiology, observing their movements, their social interactions. But this time, there was no feeling of detachment, no purely objective analysis. He felt a connection, a sense of wonder that transcended his scientific curiosity. This wasn't merely data collection; it was an encounter with something truly extraordinary. Something that defied explanation, something that confirmed the existence of magic within the heart of the Scottish Highlands. He had found them, guided not by scientific methodology, but by the whispers of the wind and the enigmatic clues of a wise old shepherd.

He spent several hours observing the Haggis, documenting their behavior in his notebook, his initial awe gradually giving way to a deep sense of respect for these extraordinary creatures. The setting sun cast a magical glow on the valley, bathing the landscape in a golden light. The wind whistled a gentle tune, carrying with it the scent of peat smoke and a faint aroma of deep-fried... haggis. He chuckled to himself, realizing that perhaps the legends held a kernel of truth after all. The mystery, however, was far from solved. The riddle pointed towards a much deeper secret, a connection between these creatures, the land,

and something far more magical than he could have ever imagined. The journey, it seemed, was just beginning.

Chapter 3

Whispers on the Wind

Following the Whispers

The wind, a mischievous sprite, tugged at Lachlan's tweed jacket as he navigated the increasingly treacherous terrain. The whispers, initially faint as the murmur of a distant stream, had grown stronger, a persistent hum resonating in the very bones of the ancient landscape. They weren't audible whispers, not in the traditional sense. They were more like… a feeling. A tingling sensation at the edge of perception, urging him onward, deeper into the heart of the Highlands. His trusty map, a faded parchment more prone to crumbling than offering clear directions, offered little help. The riddles, once deciphered, only led to more riddles, a frustrating game of Highland hide-and-seek orchestrated by some unseen, possibly haggis-shaped, hand.

Lachlan, ever the methodical zoologist, meticulously documented every twist and turn of the path, every rustle in the heather, every suspicious glint of sunlight on a distant loch. His notebook, now thick with scribbled notes, sketches of oddly shaped rocks, and what he hoped were accurate depictions of various Highland flora, served as his chronicle of this increasingly bizarre quest. He'd even started a new section entitled "Potential Haggis Habitats Based on Observed Shortbread Crumb Distribution," a testament to his unwavering dedication, bordering on obsession.

The landscape shifted and changed with every step. One moment, he was traversing a carpet of vibrant purple heather, the air thick with the scent of wild thyme and damp earth. The next, he was battling through a thicket of thorny gorse, its yellow blossoms a deceptive contrast to the sharpness of its spines. He'd already sustained a few minor injuries: a grazed knee, a scratched hand, and a surprisingly deep gash on his pride from a particularly assertive thistle. Each scrape, each stumble, only fueled his determination. The whispers, after all, were getting louder.

As dusk settled, painting the sky in hues of fiery orange and deep violet, Lachlan found himself perched on a windswept hill overlooking a valley shrouded in mist. The silence, broken only by the mournful cry of a distant curlew and the whispering wind, was profound. It was in this moment, amidst the stark beauty of the Highlands, that Lachlan felt a shift in the air, a subtle change in the energy surrounding him. The whispers intensified, no longer a mere feeling, but a tangible presence, guiding him towards a hidden pathway barely visible beneath the heather.

Following the almost invisible trail, Lachlan descended into the valley, the mist swirling around him like a ghostly shroud. The air grew colder, a damp chill clinging to his skin, and the scent of peat smoke hung heavy in the air. He emerged into a small clearing, nestled amongst ancient trees, their branches gnarled and twisted like the limbs of ancient beings. In the center of the clearing, half-hidden by the mist and the shadows of the trees, stood a circle of standing stones.

These weren't just any standing stones. These were ancient, imposing monoliths, radiating an aura of age and mystery. Runes, etched deep into their surfaces, seemed to writhe and shift under the dim light, almost as if they were alive. Lachlan, despite his scientific training, felt a shiver run down his spine. This was no ordinary place. This felt... sacred.

He cautiously approached the stones, his fingers tracing the cool, smooth surfaces of the ancient rock. As his hand brushed against one particular stone, a low hum resonated through his body, a vibration that seemed to emanate from the very earth itself. The whispers intensified, converging into a single, clear message: "The keepers await."

The keepers? Lachlan had read about them in his well-worn copy of "Scottish Folklore for the Perplexed." A secret society, shrouded in myth and legend, dedicated to the protection of the Haggis. He'd dismissed them as mere folklore, a fanciful tale spun by generations of storytellers. As he stood in the hallowed glade, enveloped by the tangible aura of the boulders, he couldn't escape the overwhelming sense of modesty, a hint of trepidation, and a burgeoning assurance that his journey was far from complete.

He spent the next hour painstakingly examining the stones, deciphering the runes with the help of his (admittedly dusty) copy of "A Beginner's Guide to Ancient Celtic Script." The runes, when translated, revealed a cryptic passage, a series of instructions that seemed to guide him towards another, even more hidden location. The message spoke of a "hidden glen," a "whispering stream," and a "cave of secrets." The instructions were vague, relying heavily on symbolism and metaphor, but Lachlan, fueled by adrenaline and a renewed sense of purpose, was determined to follow them.

As the first rays of dawn touched the horizon, casting a golden glow over the valley, Lachlan set off again, the whispers now a constant companion guiding him through the mist and the shadows. He felt a strange sense of urgency, a feeling that he was being watched, that something – or someone – was waiting for him.

The path led him through a maze of winding trails, past babbling brooks and hidden waterfalls. The air grew thicker, the scent of damp earth and decaying leaves filling his nostrils. He could hear the distant murmur of a stream, the "whispering stream" mentioned in the runes. Following the sound, he emerged into another clearing, this one even more secluded than the last.

Nestled amongst the trees, hidden from view, was a cave. Its entrance, partially concealed by a curtain of ivy, looked dark and mysterious, promising untold secrets within. As Lachlan approached, he noticed a faint glimmer of light emanating from its depths. The whispers, now a powerful force urging him forward, intensified, leaving no doubt in his mind that he was finally approaching his goal. The cave, he realized, was not merely a physical location. It was a gateway to a world unknown, a world where the legend of the Haggis might finally be revealed.

The anticipation was almost unbearable. His heart pounded in his chest, a frantic drumbeat against the backdrop of the whispering wind. He took a deep breath, steeling himself for whatever awaited him within the cave. He reached out, his hand hovering over the curtain of ivy, ready to enter the darkness… and go on to the next stage of his incredible adventure. The whispers, however, suddenly changed, their tone becoming less insistent, more… cautious. A new element had entered the equation, something unexpected, something that would dramatically alter the course of his journey. A shadow moved at the edge of the clearing. A figure, cloaked and hooded, emerged. Lachlan wasn't alone. The scent of danger lingered in the air, a hint of fear mixed with the sweet aroma of nature. His senses were on high alert, ready for the unexpected twist in his journey.

A Night Under the Stars

The cloaked figure remained silent, a dark silhouette against the rapidly darkening sky. Lachlan, momentarily thrown by the unexpected company, found himself strangely unafraid. The air, thick with the scent of peat and heather, held a different kind of whisper now, one of shared anticipation, perhaps even... camaraderie? The feeling was unsettling, yet strangely comforting. He decided against a hasty retreat; curiosity, that age-old nemesis of common sense, had firmly taken hold.

The figure gestured towards a small, sheltered cleft in the rock face, its mouth barely visible behind a curtain of ivy. It wasn't an invitation exactly, more a suggestion, an unspoken agreement to share the stillness of the approaching night. Lachlan, ever the adventurous zoologist, nodded once, his heart still thrumming a restless rhythm. He followed the figure into the small alcove, the air turning cooler, damper. The whispers, once vibrant, now faded into a low hum, a quiet conversation between the wind and the ancient stones.

The cloaked figure, finally revealing itself to be a wizened old woman with eyes as blue as a Highland loch and a smile as crooked as a shepherd's crook, produced a flask. "A dram?" she offered, her voice raspy, like the screech of a raven. Lachlan, never one to refuse a good dram, especially after a day spent chasing riddles through the Highlands, accepted the offering gratefully. The liquid burned pleasantly as it went down, chasing away the chill that had begun to seep into his bones.

"You seek the Haggis, eh?" She chuckled, a dry, rattling sound.

Lachlan, surprised by her directness, nodded. "Yes. I've been following whispers, riddles... you wouldn't believe the trouble I've gone to."

The old woman took a long sip from her own flask. "Aye, the Haggis are elusive creatures. They don't reveal themselves easily. They favour those who show respect for the land, for the whispers of the wind, for the ancient ways."

She paused, gazing up at the star-studded sky, a tapestry woven with celestial threads. "The stars hold their secrets too," she murmured, her voice barely audible above the gentle sigh of the wind. "Tonight, they whisper of patience, of persistence, of the unexpected turns fate can take. Your journey is far from over, young man. You have more to learn."

Lachlan spent the night nestled in the alcove, the old woman keeping him company with stories of the Highlands – tales of mischievous kelpies, stubborn banshees, and of course, the elusive Haggis. Her stories weren't just folklore; they were woven with the very fabric of the land, each anecdote painted with the scents of heather and peat, the taste of the whisky, and the crisp bite of the Highland air. She spoke of a time before fences and roads, when the land was wild and free, and the Haggis roamed without fear, their wool as soft as clouds, their eyes like polished jet.

The night was filled with the symphony of the Highlands. The wind whispered secrets to the heather, the stars twinkled like mischievous eyes, and the occasional hoot of an owl pierced the silence. Lachlan found himself completely

captivated, lost in the magic of the moment. He'd expected a chase, a thrilling hunt, but this... this was different. This was a communion with the land, a quiet understanding that transcended the quest itself.

As the first rays of dawn touched the horizon, painting the sky in hues of rose and gold, the old woman rose, her silhouette once again cloaked in the fading darkness. She left without a word, disappearing as silently as she'd arrived, leaving Lachlan alone with the echoes of her tales and the renewed certainty of his purpose. He wasn't just looking for a creature; he was searching for a connection, a deeper understanding of the land, of its mysteries, of its hidden heart.

The following day was spent exploring the area with a new sense of purpose. He no longer rushed; he moved with a measured pace, his senses heightened, attuned to the subtle whispers of the wind, the rustle of the heather, the faintest of scents carried on the breeze. He learned to identify the subtle nuances of the landscape, the ancient pathways carved by sheep, the hidden hollows where rabbits made their burrows. He even dared to sample a few unusual berries, only to discover a surprising burst of tart flavour. The day unfolded at a gentler rhythm than before, and the search for the Haggis somehow became less about the creature and more about the journey.

In the late afternoon, after a picnic lunch of oatcakes and cheese (the cheese, thankfully, not as pungent as the one he'd encountered in the pub earlier), he noticed something. A small, almost imperceptible movement in the heather. He held his breath, his heart pounding, not with panic, but with a joyful anticipation. He approached cautiously, his eyes scanning the landscape, his senses on high alert.

It wasn't a grand, dramatic revelation. There was no sudden appearance of a majestic Haggis herd. Instead, he saw a small family, no more than three or four, grazing peacefully amongst the heather. Their wool, a blend of deep browns and greys, blended seamlessly with the landscape. They weren't the monstrous creatures of legend, but rather, small, endearing creatures, their eyes bright and curious. They were observing him with a quiet grace, their movements delicate and precise.

Lachlan felt a profound sense of peace. The whispers had led him here, not to a confrontation, but to an understanding. The Haggis weren't a prize to be captured, but rather guardians of the Highlands, their very existence a testament to the wild beauty of the land. Their presence wasn't about mystery or magic, it was simply about their being a part of the delicate tapestry of life.

The encounter wasn't a grand climax, not with trumpets and fanfare, but a quiet, tender moment of connection. He watched them for a while, mesmerized by their gentle movements, their quiet grace, their perfect harmony with their surroundings. He didn't try to approach them, didn't try to capture them, or even to touch them. He quietly watched them, allowing their existence to overwhelm him with reverence and amazement. He knew that this was a moment he would cherish, a secret shared between him and the Highlands, a secret woven into the fabric of his memory.As dusk descended, casting long shadows across the heather, Lachlan felt a sense of contentment he'd never known before. His quest hadn't ended in the way he'd expected, but it had ended in a way that was far more profound, far more meaningful. He'd found something far greater than a legendary creature; he'd found a connection to the land, a connection to the whispers of the wind, a connection to the heart of the Highlands.

The whispers continued, but now, they were whispers of peace, of contentment, of a journey's end and the beginning of a deeper understanding. The stars above twinkled their approval, their light reflecting in the dew-kissed heather, creating a magical scene that would forever be etched in his memory. He knew, with absolute certainty, that he would carry the memory of the night, of the old woman, and of the quiet grace of the Haggis family, within his heart forever. He'd experienced something far more extraordinary than the mere discovery of a legendary beast; he'd discovered the true magic of the Scottish Highlands, a magic that whispered its secrets to those who were willing to listen, to observe, and to truly connect with the heart of the land. And as he walked away, leaving the peaceful family of Haggis to their evening meal, he knew his journey, although completed in a way he never anticipated, was ultimately a success. The whispers had led him home, not just geographically, but spiritually. His heart was full of the wild beauty of the Scottish Highlands. The Haggis, those elusive guardians of the hills, had shown him the greatest secret of all – the enduring magic of nature and the power of quiet contemplation. The journey itself, with all its twists and turns, had become its own reward, more meaningful than the outcome he'd initially envisioned. The real treasure wasn't the Haggis, but the journey itself. The whispers, the night under the stars, and the quiet understanding that came with it – this was the true essence of his Highland adventure.

The Mysterious Stone Circle

The next morning dawned bright and crisp, a stark contrast to the mystical twilight of his Haggis encounter. Lachlan, still buzzing from his surreal experience, felt a renewed sense of purpose. He'd found the Haggis, yes, but the whispers of the previous night hinted at something more, a deeper mystery woven into the very fabric of the Highlands. He'd decided to explore the area further, fuelled by a potent blend of Highland single malt and unquenchable curiosity.

His breakfast – a rather dubious-looking sausage roll acquired from a suspiciously cheerful roadside vendor –provided little sustenance for the day ahead. However, his spirits remained high. He'd packed a thermos of remarkably strong tea, a crucial element in any Scottish adventure, and a hefty supply of shortbread, the perfect companion for contemplative moments amidst breathtaking scenery.

He followed a barely discernible sheep track, his trusty walking boots crunching on the heather. The landscape unfolded before him in a panorama of rolling hills, their emerald slopes punctuated by the occasional craggy outcrop. The wind, a constant companion in the Highlands, whispered secrets only the mountains seemed to understand. Occasionally, a majestic red deer would lift its head, its antlers like branches reaching for the sky, before disappearing back into the heather's embrace. Lachlan was overcome with awe, stopping intermittently to admire the breathtaking splendor surrounding him and sensing a near transcendental bond with the earth beneath his feet.

Then, as he rounded a particularly stubborn clump of gorse, he saw it: a stone circle, seemingly emerging from the earth itself. It wasn't grand or imposing like Stonehenge, but it held a quiet dignity, a sense of ancient mystery that sent a shiver down his spine. The stones, weathered smooth by centuries of wind and rain, stood in an imperfect circle, some leaning precariously, others lying prostrate on the ground like fallen giants. Sunlight glinted off their surfaces, revealing intricate carvings that seemed almost too delicate to have survived the passage of time.

Lachlan approached cautiously, a sense of Incredible fear.mixing with apprehension. He circled the stones, his fingers tracing the weathered surfaces. The carvings were unlike anything he'd ever seen, a blend of abstract shapes and symbols that seemed to pulsate with an inner energy. He noticed a recurring motif: a small, stylized figure resembling a... haggis?

A low chuckle escaped his lips. Could this be it? The key to understanding the Haggis, their mysterious ways, their hidden history? He spent hours meticulously documenting the carvings, sketching them in his notebook, taking photographs with his ancient, slightly temperamental camera (which had, surprisingly, survived the rigors of his trip so far). He even attempted a rubbing of one particularly intriguing carving, which resulted in a smudge of charcoal and a considerable amount of frustration.

As the sun began to dip towards the horizon, painting the sky in hues of fiery orange and deep purple, Lachlan felt a strange energy emanating from the stones. It wasn't unpleasant, more like a gentle hum, a vibration that resonated deep within his bones. He closed his eyes, letting the wind carry his thoughts, his senses attuned to the whispers of the ancient stones.

He imagined the people who had built this circle, their lives, their beliefs, their connection to the land. He envisioned ancient rituals, ceremonies performed under the watchful gaze of the stars, a deep communion between humanity and nature. He pictured a community living in harmony with the haggis, perhaps even venerating them as sacred creatures. The idea wasn't so far-fetched, considering the reverence the local villagers seemed to hold for the elusive beasts.

Suddenly, a gust of wind rustled through the heather, carrying with it the faint scent of peat smoke and... haggis? Lachlan opened his eyes, his heart pounding in his chest. He looked around, but saw nothing. Had he imagined it?

Or was the stone circle truly revealing its secrets?

Determined to uncover the truth, Lachlan decided to spend the night near the circle. He set up his tent, a rather flimsy affair that offered little protection against the elements, but it was better than nothing. He built a small fire, its flames dancing in the twilight, casting long, flickering shadows across the stones. He brewed a cup of tea, the warmth a comfort against the encroaching chill.

As darkness enveloped him, the whispers returned. They weren't the gentle murmurs of the previous night, but something more intense, more urgent. They seemed to emanate from the stones themselves, a chorus of voices weaving a tale across the centuries. He could hear the sounds of ancient rituals, the chanting of voices, the beating of drums, the bleating of haggis – yes, definitely haggis. It was utterly surreal, a symphony of the past playing out in the present.

The whispers spoke of a prophecy, an ancient legend foretelling the return of a great haggis king. This king, they said, would lead his people to a new era of prosperity, restoring their ancient harmony with the land. The prophecy also spoke of a chosen one, a "keeper of the whispers," who would guide the haggis king to his rightful place. Could Lachlan, the slightly bewildered zoologist from New Zealand, be this chosen one?

The thought was absurd, yet strangely compelling. He felt a strong connection to the stones, to the land, to the elusive haggis. It was as if the stone circle, the whispers, and the haggis themselves were all interconnected, part of a grand, cosmic tapestry.

As the night wore on, the whispers intensified, weaving a more intricate narrative. They described a hidden passage, a secret pathway leading to the haggis's sacred domain. The pathway, they said, was concealed beneath the largest stone in the circle, a massive boulder that had lain undisturbed for centuries. The whispers indicated that this stone could only be moved by someone with a pure heart, someone who understood and respected the ancient ways.

Sunrise painted the sky in vibrant hues, ending the night of intense revelations. Lachlan, exhausted but exhilarated, felt a surge of newfound purpose. He had to move the stone. He had to find the hidden passage. He had to fulfill the prophecy, even if it meant wrestling a giant boulder in the early morning light, all while battling a hangover from a suspiciously potent blend of single malt and ancient Highland magic.

The task seemed daunting, even impossible, but Lachlan wasn't one to back down from a challenge, especially not one involving a potential haggis king. He approached the largest stone, taking a deep breath, and summoning all his strength, both physical and spiritual. He braced himself, and with a grunt that would have done a Highland games competitor proud, he pushed. The stone shifted, revealing a dark, narrow opening beneath. The whispers, now softer, gentler, seemed to be guiding him onward.

His adventure, it seemed, was far from over. The stone circle, a silent sentinel of the ages, had opened its secrets to him. The journey to find the haggis king had become a quest of far greater significance, a journey into the heart of ancient magic, a pilgrimage into the soul of the Highlands. And Lachlan McGregor, the somewhat bewildered zoologist, was about to step into the unknown. His trusty thermos of tea, however, remained firmly by his side, a source of both comfort and inspiration in the face of whatever marvels, or minor inconveniences, lay ahead. The adventure continued, richer and more profound than he could have ever imagined. The whispers, once faint and distant, now resonated loud and clear, leading him deeper into the heart of the Highland mystery. He stepped into the dark opening, the scent of peat smoke and haggis strong in the air, ready for the next chapter of his extraordinary tale.

The Legend of the Haggis Keepers

The air hung thick with the scent of peat and something vaguely...haggis-y. Lachlan, his tweed jacket damp from the Highland mist, found himself in a cavern surprisingly spacious considering its unassuming entrance. The walls were illuminated by flickering torches, their ethereal glow casting dancing shadows. As Lachlan gazed upon the rough carvings, he could not decipher their meaning. They seemed to be a bizarre blend of haggis, bagpipes, and what might have been particularly disgruntled-looking cabbages.

He ventured deeper, the whispers he'd heard the previous night growing stronger, weaving themselves into the very texture of the stone. They weren't whispers of wind anymore; these were whispers of secrets, old and deeply buried. The air vibrated with a low hum, a sound that resonated deep within his chest, a strange counterpoint to the rhythmic drip, drip, drip of water echoing from unseen depths.

Suddenly, the cavern opened into a vast chamber. In the center, around a crackling fire that cast an orange glow on everything, sat a group of people. They weren't your average Highland folk. These individuals, clad in robes of deep purple and adorned with curious silver brooches shaped like miniature haggis, radiated an air of quiet authority. They were... dignified, even imposing, but there was also an underlying air of playful mischief in their eyes.

Lachlan, ever the cautious zoologist, approached slowly, his trusty thermos of tea clutched tightly in his hand. "Good evening," he ventured, his voice echoing slightly in the cavernous space. "I trust I haven't intruded?"

A woman with a surprisingly bright pink streak in her otherwise grey hair rose from the circle. She possessed a gaze that could simultaneously melt glaciers and curdle milk. "Intruded?" she said, a smile playing on her lips. "My dear Mr. McGregor, we've been expecting you."

Lachlan blinked. "Expecting me? But... how?"

"The whispers," she replied, gesturing towards a particularly flamboyant haggis-brooch wearer. "Angus here is rather...vocal. He's been quite insistent on your arrival. A bit like a persistent, furry bagpipe, really."

Angus, a man of considerable girth and an even more considerable beard, merely grunted in agreement. He then proceeded to take a surprisingly large bite from a rather impressive-looking haggis. It was a performance, Lachlan realised. These people were masters of theatrics.

"You see," the pink-haired woman continued, "we are the Keepers of the Haggis. A secret society, dedicated to the preservation and... well, the general well-being of the Haggis population."

Lachlan's jaw dropped. "A secret society?" he

breathed. "Dedicated to haggis?"

"Indeed," another Keeper, a wizened old man with eyes that twinkled like distant stars, chimed in. "For centuries, we have guarded the Haggis, ensuring their safety and prosperity. We've faced down Nessie's disgruntled cousins, outwitted grumpy giants, and even negotiated peace treaties with particularly territorial badgers."

"Badgers?" Lachlan queried, bewildered. "Badgers and Haggis? What's the connection?"

The old man chuckled. "Ah, my boy, you have much to learn. The Highland ecosystem is a delicate dance of inter-species rivalry and unexpected alliances. The badger, you see, has a particular fondness for the finest Haggis root vegetables."

Lachlan scribbled furiously in his notebook, his earlier skepticism evaporating. This was far beyond anything he'd ever encountered in his career. This wasn't just about zoology; it was about folklore, history, and a level of Highland eccentricity that defied all logical explanation.

The Keepers then proceeded to regale Lachlan with the history of their society. It stretched back to the mists of time, a tapestry woven with tales of brave haggis heroes, cunning strategies to protect their beloved creatures from poachers (who, surprisingly, mostly turned out to be disgruntled chefs), and ingenious methods of haggis husbandry.

Lachlan learned of the Haggis King, a majestic creature said to possess the wisdom of the ages and the ability to communicate with the very stones of the Highlands. He heard tales of the annual Haggis Games, a series of fiercely competitive events involving haggis-hurling, haggis-herding, and haggis-based culinary challenges that put even the most seasoned chef to shame. The culinary challenges, he learned, involved intense levels of haggis-related creativity that bordered on the avant-garde. One Keeper, a young woman with a mischievous grin and an impressive collection of haggis-themed earrings, described a particularly memorable contest involving haggis-shaped soufflés and a judging panel that included a very opinionated Highland cow.

They discussed the complex social hierarchy of the Haggis, its intricate communication system (mostly involving a series of grunts, squeaks and surprisingly eloquent bellows), and the intricate rituals involved in their mating dances (apparently, involving a lot of skillful leaping and a surprising amount of synchronized head-bobbing). They even showed Lachlan ancient scrolls detailing the correct way to make a Haggis-based potion for curing the common cold (involving equal parts honey, heather, and surprisingly, a single strand of a Haggis's whisker).

As the night wore on, the fire dwindled, the torches flickered, and the stories flowed. Lachlan, initially skeptical, was now completely captivated. He was no longer just a zoologist;

he was an honorary Keeper of the Haggis, a member of this extraordinary community, entrusted with their secrets. He felt a sense of responsibility towards these fascinating creatures, a feeling far deeper than mere scientific curiosity.

He learned about the threats facing the Haggis, not just from the usual suspects (disgruntled chefs and overly enthusiastic badger populations), but from the encroaching modern world. Tourism, industrial development, and the relentless march of progress were all taking their toll on the fragile ecosystem that supported these magnificent creatures. The Keepers were struggling to maintain the balance.

Before he left, the pink-haired woman, whose name he learned was Morag, handed him a small, intricately carved wooden box. "This," she said, "contains a single Haggis whisker. Keep it safe. It holds the essence of the Highlands, the spirit of the Haggis, and a tiny bit of our secret magic.

"Lachlan accepted the box, a profound sense of gratitude and wonder filling his heart. His journey had taken him far beyond the realm of scientific exploration. It had brought him to the heart of a timeless legend, to a place where the mystical and the mundane intertwined, where the whispers of the wind carried secrets of an ancient brotherhood, dedicated to the protection of a culinary marvel that had captured the imagination of a world. His adventure wasn't over; it had only just begun. He had a whisker to protect, a legend to uphold, and a whole lot of haggis-related mysteries to unravel. And, he realised, he wouldn't have it any other way. The journey home would be filled with new stories, the taste of Highland hospitality, and the lingering scent of peat and... well, you know.

Unexpected Company

The cavern mouth, barely visible behind a curtain of dripping ferns, seemed to sigh as Lachlan emerged, clutching the small, exquisitely carved wooden box containing the whisker. The Highland night had deepened, the stars blazing with an almost aggressive brilliance against the inky sky. He took a deep breath, the crisp air a welcome change from the earthy aroma of the cavern. He was about to set off on the trek back to his borrowed cottage when a sound, a peculiar blend of rustling heather and muffled giggles, caught his attention.

Peeking around a particularly gnarled oak, Lachlan discovered the source of the commotion. It was a gathering, a truly bizarre assembly of individuals that defied any logical explanation. First, there was Agnes, a woman whose age was as indeterminate as the number of shawls she wore. Each shawl, it seemed, boasted a different shade of tartan, a kaleidoscope of Highland hues that threatened to overwhelm the senses. Agnes, perched on a moss-covered boulder, was intensely engaged in a game of something that resembled three-card monte, only with miniature haggis figurines instead of cards.

Her opponent was a man named Angus, a giant of a fellow whose beard flowed down to his waist like a tangled river of peat and whisky. Angus, clad in a kilt that seemed to be fashioned from an army surplus of brightly colored plaids, possessed an air of jovial menace. He was losing badly, his face a mask of comical despair as Agnes swept another haggis figurine into her winning pile.

Observing them with a mixture of amusement and bewilderment was Morag, a woman whose wardrobe seemed to consist entirely of tweed jackets. She had at least five on at once, each layered over the other, creating a sort of human tweed-burrito effect. Morag was muttering incantations under her breath – or perhaps they were recipes; it was hard to tell. They involved copious amounts of oatmeal, a surprising number of onions, and what sounded suspiciously like a recipe for dynamite.

Then there was Hamish, a small, wiry man who seemed to be constructed entirely of twigs and enthusiasm. He wore a tam-o'-shanter that was precariously perched on his head and carried a bagpipe that appeared to be older than the hills themselves. Hamish, oblivious to the chaos surrounding him, was attempting to coax a tune from his instrument, producing a sound that could only be described as a distressed badger attempting to sing opera.

Lachlan, cautiously approaching, cleared his throat. The quartet stopped their various activities and stared at him with a mixture of surprise, suspicion, and – dare he say it? – expectation.

"Good evening," Lachlan ventured, feeling a sudden urge to apologize for interrupting their rather unique game of haggis-based chance.

Agnes, without missing a beat, swept a haggis figurine into her pile, declaring, "Another one for the wee granny! Now, you look like a man who's just come from that place. The Whispering Cavern!" Her voice was surprisingly strong for someone who appeared to be woven entirely from wool.

"Yes," Lachlan replied, somewhat startled by her prescience. "That's right. I... I found something rather remarkable in there." He held up the box carefully, revealing a glimpse of the polished wood.

Angus, whose despair had momentarily been forgotten in the appearance of a new person, bellowed, "Remarkable? What is it? Is it... more haggis? Because I'm feeling rather peckish."

Morag, still muttering about onions and potentially explosive ingredients, looked up with a flicker of suspicion. "He's one of the Whispers Keepers, isn't he?" she muttered to Agnes, who simply winked. "One of those blessed fools who believes in the legend."

Hamish, having finally coaxed a semi-coherent note from his bagpipes, added, "Aye, he carries the mark of the Haggis Whisperer. I can smell it in his tweeds! It's faintly reminiscent of... overcooked turnips."

Lachlan, slightly overwhelmed, stammered, "I'm... I'm Lachlan McGregor. A zoologist. I was researching..." He trailed off, realizing he'd made a terrible first impression on the most eccentric group of individuals ever assembled on a Scottish hillside.

Agnes chuckled, a sound like dry leaves skittering across a stone floor. "Researcher, eh? Well, you've certainly found yourselves in the right place. We've been expecting you."

This, he thought, could either be fantastic news or a potential prelude to his demise. He decided to focus on the fantastic aspect. With the help of such uniquely qualified guides, finding the answer to the question of the Haggis wouldn't be a question of if, but ofhow much mischiefwould they cause along the way.

Over the next few hours, Lachlan learned far more about the Haggis and its mysterious guardians than he ever could have imagined. Angus, it turned out, was a retired champion caber-tosser who believed he could communicate with haggis through interpretive dance (a talent he demonstrated with alarming enthusiasm). Morag, who claimed to be a seventh-generation haggis-whisperer, divulged secret recipes and potent spells for dealing with recalcitrant haggis (and presumably, also recalcitrant Scots). Hamish, despite his less-than-perfect piping skills, knew the history of the haggis brotherhood better than anyone, recounting tales of daring haggis rescues and epic battles against rogue sheepdogs.

Agnes, the enigmatic leader of this unlikely fellowship, proved to be a master strategist and storyteller. She revealed the lore surrounding the Haggis: their surprisingly complex social structure, their peculiar fondness for bagpipes, and their uncanny ability to predict the weather. She also shared the secret locations of the best haggis-related landmarks: Haggis-shaped rocks, Whispering Haggis Holes, and the legendary Haggis-themed pub, "The Wee Haggis's Hideaway."

Their night progressed under the watchful gaze of the stars. Lachlan, initially apprehensive, found himself captivated by their strange, wonderful world. He shared his own research, and much to his surprise, found a surprisingly receptive audience. He discovered that his scientific approach, though initially met with some suspicion, ultimately meshed with their lore, weaving a tapestry of fact and fantasy.

The stories flowed like the whisky, warm and inviting, each one more fantastical than the last. Lachlan learned about the annual Haggis Migration, a spectacular event where

hundreds of haggis would journey across the Highlands, following ancient routes known only to the brotherhood. He heard tales of haggis possessing remarkable skills in disguise and their penchant for elaborate pranks. They also had a secret language, a series of squeaks and whistles only understood by the initiated.

As the first rays of dawn kissed the hills, painting the heather in shades of gold and purple, Lachlan knew his journey had reached another unexpected turning point. He wasn't simply a researcher anymore. He was an honorary member of the Haggis Brotherhood, a keeper of secrets, a confidante of the quirky, the mysterious and the wonderfully, gloriously

strange. The road ahead was as uncertain as ever, filled with mysteries and perhaps more mishaps, but one thing was certain: He would face them all with these eccentric

companions by his side. And he already knew that the tales of their adventures would be far more legendary than any haggis-related legend he'd ever heard. The smell of peat, whisky, and slightly overcooked turnips hung sweetly in the morning air, a testament to a night of unlikely friendships and even more unlikely stories. The quest for the Haggis was far from over. Indeed, it had just begun, and what a journey it promised to be.

Chaper 4

A Drunken Revelation

The LateNight Pub Crawl

The air in the "Whisky Whisperer" pub hung thick with the aroma of peat smoke, spilled ale, and a faint, indefinable scent that Lachlan initially attributed to the questionable hygiene of a particularly boisterous patron. He'd been chasing the Haggis legend for weeks, his initial scientific rigour slowly dissolving into a desperate, almost drunken, pursuit. His carefully-constructed algorithm, predicting Haggis migration patterns based on shortbread consumption, had yielded nothing but a throbbing headache and a rapidly depleting supply of Scotch. Tonight, however, felt different. A palpable shift in the energy of the pub, a subtle hum in the air, hinted at something... significant.

Angus, the bartender – a man whose age was as debatable as the existence of the Haggis itself – poured Lachlan another dram, the amber liquid shimmering under the dim lighting. "Ye still lookin' for tha' wee beastie, are ye?" he rumbled, his voice like gravel gargling with whisky.

Lachlan nodded, his resolve momentarily wavering under the weight of the accumulated disappointment. He'd interviewed shepherds who spoke in riddles, consulted fortune tellers whose predictions were less than illuminating, and even attempted to communicate with a particularly grumpy Highland cow, who seemed more interested in chewing on his notes than offering helpful advice.

"Aye," he replied, his voice slightly slurred, "and I'm about ready to give up and write a book about my failures. A bestseller, of course." He chuckled, the sound a little too forced.

Angus chuckled back, a deep, throaty sound that seemed to shake the very foundations of the pub. "Failures? Nonsense! The Haggis don't reveal their secrets tae just anyone. Ye need... a certain... persuasion." He winked conspiratorially, and Lachlan's curiosity piqued. The conversation meandered into a discussion about local lore, interspersed with anecdotes involving questionable sheep-herding techniques and an unfortunate incident involving a rogue bagpipe and a flock of startled geese.

By the time the pub began to empty, Lachlan found himself engaged in a rather heated debate with a group of locals about the precise aerodynamic properties of a thrown haggis (a topic, it turned out, that generated surprisingly intense opinions). The argument was punctuated by bursts of laughter, copious amounts of whisky, and the occasional rendition of a rather off-key Gaelic drinking song.

As the last strains of the song faded, Angus leaned in, his voice dropping to a conspiratorial whisper. "Follow the stream," he said, "past the whispering stones. But heed my warning, lad. The Haggis are shy creatures. They'll only show themselves to those who are.. . receptive." He tapped a knowing finger to his temple, his words hanging in the air like the lingering aroma of peat.

Lachlan, fortified by copious amounts of whisky and the potent mixture of local lore and speculation, stumbled out into the night. The moon cast long, skeletal shadows across the heather-covered hills. The air was crisp and cool, carrying the scent of damp earth and a faint, almost imperceptible aroma of... something strangely familiar. He followed the stream, the gurgling water a lullaby to his slightly unsteady gait. The whispering stones, as Angus had described, were indeed whispering. Not with words, but with a subtle rustling, a low hum that vibrated in his very bones.

His path led him through a maze of twisting paths, his steps becoming increasingly erratic as the effects of the whisky intensified. He tripped over a gnarled root, tumbling head over heels into a patch of heather. He landed with a surprised grunt, a soft sigh escaping his lips.

But as he lay there, dazed but not entirely incapacitated, he saw it. A small clearing, nestled amongst the heather, bathed in the silvery light of the moon. And there, within the clearing, was a family of Haggis.

They were nothing like the culinary concoction he'd anticipated. These were small, furry creatures, vaguely resembling oversized guinea pigs with exceptionally fluffy tails. They were huddled together, their eyes gleaming with an intelligence that surprised Lachlan. Their fur was a patchwork of browns and greys, perfectly camouflaged against the heather. They were chattering amongst themselves in a high-pitched squeak, their movements surprisingly agile and graceful.

Lachlan watched them, captivated. His scientific curiosity, temporarily overshadowed by the whisky, reasserted itself.

He reached for his notebook, carefully documenting their behaviour, their interactions, their remarkable ability to blend seamlessly with their surroundings. He sketched their charmingly awkward gait, their surprisingly expressive faces. He even managed to capture a few blurry photographs before his clumsy fingers fumbled with the camera.

One of the Haggis, bolder than the others, approached him cautiously. It sniffed at his outstretched hand, its tiny nose twitching. Lachlan froze, his heart pounding in his chest. The little creature seemed unafraid. It rested its head against his hand, its soft fur brushing against his skin.

In that moment, under the silent gaze of the moon and the watchful eyes of the Haggis family, Lachlan felt a connection to the creatures. He understood their shyness, their need for protection, the reasons behind the locals'secrecy. They were not just a legendary creature; they were a vital part of the Highlands, a sign of the magic that lay hidden in the heart of the Scottish landscape. He realized Angus's words weren't just a drunken riddle; it was the truth, revealed only to someone open to receiving it. The late-night pub crawl hadn't just led to a drunken revelation; it was a transformative experience.

He had found more than just a mythical creature; he had found a connection, a respect, and a responsibility. The secrets of the Haggis would remain safe with him, guarded with the same reverence as he guarded the newfound respect he felt for the whisky-fueled wisdom of the Scottish Highlands.

A Stumble in the Heather

The night air, thick with the scent of bog myrtle and damp earth, slapped Lachlan in the face as he stumbled from the "Whisky Whisperer," his gait more reminiscent of a drunken penguin than a world-renowned zoologist. He clutched a half-empty bottle of something suspiciously resembling battery acid – a "local delicacy," according to the barman –and mumbled apologies to the startled sheep that scattered before him. His carefully constructed algorithm, his years of academic research, had all dissolved into a hazy miasma of peat smoke and questionable single malts. Yet, a strange sense of exhilaration, fueled by questionable alcohol and a desperate hope, propelled him forward.

He'd been following a whisper, a fleeting glimpse of something furry and...haggis-shaped, darting across the moonlit moor. Angus, the pub's resident oracle (and possibly owner), had mumbled something about "following the wee beasties' trail of...digestive fortitude," a cryptic clue that only made sense after a few drams of the aforementioned battery acid. Lachlan, ever the dedicated scientist (or at least, he'd once been), had stubbornly interpreted this as a literal trail – a path paved with particularly robust sheep droppings, perhaps?

His journey through the heather was a symphony of stumbles and near-misses with unseen obstacles. He tripped over tussocks of grass the size of small dogs, narrowly avoided plunging into unseen bogs, and had a surprisingly intimate encounter with a particularly grumpy-looking badger. The badger, it appeared, had no appreciation for drunken zoologists invading its nightly foraging. It hissed, displaying teeth that could rival a particularly aggressive set of garden shears, before retreating into the inky blackness of the moor. Lachlan, equally intimidated, continued his rather inelegant progress.

The wind howled a mournful tune, whipping his already dishevelled hair across his face. He imagined the legendary Haggis, if they indeed existed, huddled together, watching his ridiculous progress with a mixture of amusement and pity. Perhaps they were even placing bets on whether he'd manage to make it to the next particularly large patch of heather without falling flat on his face.

Then, amidst a particularly dense patch of heather, a sight that would have stopped his heart, were it not already pounding a frantic rhythm against his ribs, met his eye.

A family of Haggis.

Not the plump, sausage-shaped creatures of legend, but something far more remarkable. They were small, undeniably fluffy, and possessed an air of quiet dignity that belied their rather comical appearance. Their fur was the colour of a twilight sky, tinged with the purple of the surrounding heather. They moved with a surprising grace, their small legs padding silently across the moorland. They were...adorable.

Lachlan froze, his drunken bravado momentarily replaced by awe. He watched, the Haggis family went about their evening activities. They nibbled on something that looked suspiciously like rare Highland lichen, chased each other in playful bursts of energy, and occasionally engaged in a series of high-pitched squeaks that might have been their version of conversation.

He was so captivated by the scene that he remained perfectly still, forgetting his aching limbs and the throbbing in his head. The Haggis, seemingly oblivious to his presence, continued their evening rituals. One particularly bold young Haggis, seemingly unafraid of the large, slightly smelly, and very drunk human, ventured close enough to allow Lachlan a closer look. Its fur was incredibly soft, like the finest cashmere, and its eyes held a spark of intelligence that belied its diminutive size.

For a long moment, Lachlan just watched. The initial shock and disbelief had given way to a profound sense of wonder. He understood, in that moment, the reason behind the locals' reluctance to reveal the Haggis' location. They weren't just a quirky legend; they were a fragile part of the Highland, deserving of protection and reverence.

The moon cast long, dancing shadows across the heather, adding to the surreal beauty of the moment. Lachlan realized the absurdity of his situation: a world-renowned zoologist, tipsy on questionable spirits, having a private audience with a family of mythical creatures. It was the kind of scene only a drunken stumble through the heather could possibly create.

He reached into his pocket, intending to pull

out his notebook and make a few hasty sketches – a scientist's instinct, even in a state of mild intoxication – but hesitated. He knew that any attempts to document this encounter, to subject these magnificent creatures to the cold, clinical analysis of science, would somehow diminish their magic. They were not specimens to be studied; they were creatures to be observed, and cherished.

Instead, he simply sat back, leaning against a particularly sturdy heather bush, and allowed himself to be absorbed by the scene. The night air, once biting and cold, now felt strangely comforting. The wind seemed to whisper secrets only he could understand. He spent the next hour watching the Haggis family, feeling a sense of peace descend over him. The drunken stumble through the heather had been more than just a lucky break; it was a transformative experience.

As dawn approached, painting the sky in hues of pink and orange, the Haggis began to disperse. They melted back into the heather, leaving no trace of their presence except for a lingering sense of wonder. Lachlan, now sobered by the cool morning air, felt a pang of sadness at their departure but also a deep sense of satisfaction.

He had found the Haggis, not through meticulous research or advanced algorithms, but through a happy accident, a drunken stumble, and a healthy dose of serendipity. He realized that sometimes, the most extraordinary discoveries are made not in the laboratory, but in the unexpected corners of the world, under the watchful eyes of a family of fluffy, mythical creatures, somewhere in the heart of the Scottish Highlands, where legend and reality often blurred into a beautiful, incomprehensible, whisky-scented haze. He made his way back to his lodgings, the image of the Haggis family imprinted on his mind. The memory was not just a scientific observation, but a heartwarming story, a secret he would keep. The Haggis were safe, and Lachlan, the somewhat tipsy, somewhat heroic zoologist, had fulfilled his quest in the most unexpected way imaginable.

His journey wasn't over, of course. He still had to navigate the intricacies of the local community, explain his late-night absence, and perhaps avoid mentioning the slightly incriminating nature of his discovery. But for now, he allowed himself a small smile, a happy memory, and the quiet satisfaction of a profound revelation discovered amidst a drunken stumble in the heather. The adventure had only just begun, and it was certainly going to be a memorable one, full of the kind of unexpected joys and discoveries that could only happen when one chased a legend with a bottle of questionable whiskey and a heart full of hope. The journey was a proof to the fact that even the most scientific of minds can, occasionally, benefit from a healthy dose of blind faith, drunken wandering, and a surprisingly good sense of direction, when it matters most. He chuckled softly. He'd have a story to tell, one far more interesting than any academic paper. And he had a feeling that this was only the beginning of his extraordinary adventures on the Isle of Skye. The next step was to acquire a proper map, and perhaps a less potent brand of whiskey. The quest for the Haggis might be over, but the quest for adventure was only just beginning.

The Haggis Family

The heather, normally a vibrant purple haze under the Scottish sky, now seemed to shimmer with an ethereal, almost phosphorescent glow in the pre-dawn light. Lachlan, his head throbbing in rhythm with the bleating of a distant sheep, blinked. He'd been certain he'd stumbled into a bog, a particularly unpleasant variety judging by the clinging mud coating his tweed trousers. Instead, he found himself in a small, hidden valley, a secret amphitheatre carved into the heart of the Highlands. And in the centre, a sight that made him forget his aching head and the lingering taste of battery-acid whiskey: a family of Haggis.

Not the culinary kind, of course. These were... well, they defied description. Picture, if you will, a cross between a fluffy sheepdog, a particularly plump badger, and a miniature Highland cow, all rolled into one surprisingly agile package. They were covered in a thick, shaggy coat the colour of burnt heather, their little legs surprisingly sturdy, and their eyes held a mischievous glint. They weren't the shapeless, amorphous blobs of legend, but rather, charming, if slightly eccentric, creatures.

One, a larger Haggis, seemingly the matriarch, was grooming her young, a cluster of fluffy balls of fluff who tumbled over each other with a surprising amount of energy. They resembled miniature versions of their parent, their coats still a bit patchy, like unfinished sweaters. Their movements were fluid and graceful, their short legs propelling them with surprising speed across the dewy grass. They were far from the culinary stereotype; these were animals possessing an undeniable charm and surprising intelligence.

Despite his throbbing headache, Lachlan was overcome with an immense sense of veneration.. He'd spent years studying the scientific literature, poring over dubious folklore, and consulting with eccentric historians, all in pursuit of this elusive creature. And here they were, in all their fluffy glory, looking remarkably unconcerned about the presence of a very dishevelled zoologist clutching a nearly empty bottle of questionable alcohol.

The matriarch Haggis, apparently unconcerned by his presence, let out a sound that was somewhere between a bleat and a chuckle. It was a sound that held no malice, only a sort of amused curiosity. One of the younger Haggis, bolder than its siblings, waddled towards Lachlan, sniffing at his mud-caked boots with a curious nose. It then proceeded to lick his hand, its tongue surprisingly soft and surprisingly clean. Lachlan cautiously knelt, his movements slow and deliberate. He reached out a trembling finger, and the young Haggis nuzzled it, a surprisingly gentle touch. He felt a wave of emotion wash over him – relief, joy, and a deep sense of satisfaction. His years of research had culminated in this extraordinary moment, a meeting that transcended the realms of scientific observation and entered the realm of pure, unadulterated wonder.

He spent the next few hours observing the Haggis family, carefully documenting their behaviour in his still slightly damp notebook. They were surprisingly social creatures, engaging in playful interactions amongst themselves, their movements a symphony of gentle nudges and soft bleats. They foraged for food with a surprising dexterity, their snouts rooting through the earth with an almost meditative grace.

The sun climbed higher, casting long shadows across the valley. The Haggis family, sensing the change in light, began to settle down for the day. They seemed to retreat into a network of burrows hidden amongst the rocks and heather, their movements swift and efficient. Lachlan, reluctant to disturb their peace, slowly backed away, feeling a sense of respect for these magnificent creatures.

He knew he couldn't reveal their location to just anyone. The possibility of human interference, even well-intentioned, could disrupt their delicate ecosystem. The Haggis deserved to remain hidden, a secret jewel tucked away in the heart of the Highlands. He'd need to consider the implications of his discovery carefully. Perhaps a discreet article in a specialized zoological journal, focusing on the ecological significance of their habitat, without compromising their location.

As he made his way back towards civilization, the hangover had receded, replaced by a sense of gratitude. He carried with him not only a story of drunken discovery, but also a sense of responsibility towards these extraordinary creatures. He had found his Haggis, and in doing so, he had discovered a new level of respect for the mysteries and marvels of the natural world.

The return to the village was far less eventful. He even managed to avoid encountering any more startled sheep. The local pub, the "Whisky Whisperer," seemed a little less intimidating this morning, the bartender greeting him with a raised eyebrow and a knowing smirk. Lachlan simply grinned back, his heart overflowing with a joy that no amount of hangover could diminish. He had a secret to keep, a story to carefully unfold, and a renewed sense of purpose in his life as a zoologist.

His scientific mind whirred with questions. What was their diet? How did their social structure function? What were the unique adaptations that allowed them to thrive in this seemingly harsh environment? His earlier research, focused on the mythical aspect of the Haggis, now seemed utterly inadequate. He'd need to conduct a more thorough study, a comprehensive analysis of their behavior and ecology, possibly involving advanced genetic sequencing and sophisticated camera traps, all while ensuring their safety and preserving their secluded habitat. This was no longer a whimsical quest; it was a scientific imperative.

He found himself sketching out preliminary research plans in the margins of his notebook, his pencil moving rapidly across the pages, fuelled by a combination of adrenaline, relief, and a surprisingly robust breakfast of porridge and smoked salmon. The initial excitement of the discovery gradually gave way to the methodical approach of a seasoned scientist. The story of his discovery would be interesting, indeed, but it would be far more compelling alongside the scientific data. He would present the data carefully, respecting the balance between the scientific findings and the need to protect the Haggis from human curiosity.

The news of Lachlan's return, however, spread like wildfire through the small village. His late-night escapade, originally a source of amused gossip, was quickly overshadowed by the whispers of his remarkable discovery. He found himself the subject of intense speculation, although thankfully, no one seemed particularly interested in the exact details of his alcohol-fuelled journey. They were more captivated by the prospect of a real, live Haggis.

He spent the next few days navigating the delicate balance between scientific curiosity and the need to protect his newly discovered friends. He subtly deflected the questions

regarding their location, offering vague descriptions of their habitat, stressing the importance of respecting their privacy.

In the following days, he skillfully navigated the fine line between his scientific inquisitiveness and the obligation to safeguard his newfound companions. He tactfully evaded questions about their whereabouts, providing ambiguous descriptions of their habitat and emphasizing the importance of respecting their privacy. He was aware that, despite their initial reluctance, the islanders held a profound reverence for the natural world. He appealed to this inherent understanding, reminding them of the fragile equilibrium of the Highland ecosystem.

In the end, Lachlan's story became a legend in its own right, a tale woven into the fabric of the Isle of Skye's folklore. He became a local hero, not for conquering the Haggis, but for respecting them, for understanding the importance of

protecting the extraordinary wonders that lie hidden in plain sight. His drunken stumble had, quite unexpectedly, led him to a far more profound discovery than he could ever have imagined. He had found the Haggis, but more importantly, he had found a newfound respect for the natural world and the extraordinary creatures that inhabit it. His adventure continued, though now guided by a profound sense of responsibility and a profound love for the mystical, fluffy inhabitants of the Scottish Highlands. The whiskey might have been questionable, but the discovery was undeniably extraordinary. The journey had just begun. The scientific world awaited. And the Haggis? They remained safe in their secret valley, their secret protected by a man who had initially found them under the influence of a rather potent and dubious spirit.

Observing the Haggis

The valley floor, bathed in the soft light of the nascent sun, revealed itself to be a surprisingly fertile patch. Forget the boggy misery Lachlan had anticipated; this was a miniature Eden, a tapestry woven with wildflowers of unexpected vibrancy. Tiny streams, clear as glacial meltwater, chuckled their way through the verdant landscape, feeding a small, secluded loch that mirrored the sky with unnerving accuracy. And there they were: the Haggis.

Not just one, as his bleary, whisky-addled eyes had initially perceived, but a whole family. At least half a dozen of them, ranging in size from something resembling a particularly plump guinea pig to a creature that might have challenged a small terrier for dominance. They were, undeniably, far fluffier than any textbook illustration could ever capture. Their fur, a mesmerizing blend of russet, ochre, and deepest brown, seemed to shimmer with an inner light, like spun gold catching the first rays of dawn.

Lachlan, his head still thrumming a gentle protest against the previous night's libations, reached for his trusty notebook —miraculously dry, despite his earlier misadventures. His pencil, a faithful companion on countless expeditions, felt strangely inadequate in the face of this unexpected wonder.

He started meticulously, almost reverently, documenting their movements. He noted the almost comical waddle of the larger Haggis, their stubby legs churning the soft earth with surprising efficiency. The smaller ones, in contrast, displayed an almost alarming agility, darting and weaving through the wildflowers with the speed and grace of miniature, furry ninjas.

Their feeding habits proved equally fascinating. They seemed to possess an almost preternatural ability to locate the juiciest, plumpest berries, their tiny snouts working with remarkable precision. One particularly intrepid young Haggis attempted to tackle a particularly large, suspiciously purple mushroom. The elder Haggis, a magnificent beast with a commanding presence and what Lachlan could only describe as a surprisingly dignified air, intervened with a sharp, high-pitched squeak that resembled a rusty hinge protesting its age. The mushroom was left untouched.

Lachlan was immersed in fascination for the following several hours. He observed their complex social interactions, the gentle nudges and playful nips that underscored their strong family bonds. He documented their vocalizations – a surprising range of squeaks, whistles, and the occasional rumble that hinted at subterranean communication networks, akin to prairie dogs, only far, far fluffier. He even attempted to sketch their faces, a challenge that proved surprisingly difficult. Their expressions seemed to shift constantly, from sleepy contentment to alert vigilance, with a spectrum of emotions in between that defied easy categorization.

He documented their vocalizations – a surprising range of squeaks, whistles, and the occasional rumble that hinted at subterranean communication networks, akin to prairie dogs, only far, far fluffier. He even attempted to sketch their faces, a challenge that proved surprisingly difficult. Their expressions seemed to shift constantly, from sleepy contentment to alert vigilance, with a spectrum of emotions in between that defied easy categorization.

He discovered that their fur wasn't simply fluffy; it possessed a remarkable sheen, a quality that suggested a sophisticated system of self-grooming and perhaps, the secret to their seemingly imperviousness to the harsh

Scottish weather. He pondered the implications of their peculiar diet, noting the abundance of rare herbs and fungi in their immediate vicinity, and wondered if their unusual physiology held the key to novel medicinal compounds. His scientific mind, initially subdued by the sheer strangeness of the situation, was finally kicking into high gear. As the sun climbed higher in the sky, casting long shadows across the valley, Lachlan's attention shifted from individual observation to a broader ecological assessment. The interplay between the Haggis and their environment was remarkably intricate. He noticed the strategic positioning of their burrows, skillfully camouflaged amidst the dense vegetation, offering protection from both the elements and potential predators. He observed the way the Haggis interacted with the local flora and fauna, a complex dance of mutualism and subtle competition. Their presence seemed to be integral to the valley's delicate ecosystem, a cornerstone of its biodiversity.

The implications were staggering. This wasn't just about observing a strange creature; it was about uncovering a previously unknown ecosystem, a hidden world teeming with life and secrets waiting to be revealed. The scientific community, with its rigid methodologies and often narrow focus, had completely missed this extraordinary discovery. Lachlan, fuelled by questionable whiskey and a boundless enthusiasm for the bizarre, had stumbled upon a treasure beyond measure.

He carefully collected samples of plant matter, noting their proximity to the Haggis burrows. He took soil samples, searching for evidence of unusual microbial activity. He even managed to capture a few strands of Haggis fur – a feat achieved with a surprising amount of patience and a liberal application of bribery (in the form of exceptionally juicy berries). Every detail, every observation, was meticulously documented in his notebook, a testament to his dedication and the overwhelming wonder of his discovery.

As the day wore on, a quiet understanding began to settle between Lachlan and the Haggis family. They initially displayed a healthy dose of suspicion, their eyes following his every move with an intensity that was both captivating and slightly unnerving. But as he proved his non-threatening intentions through quiet observation and a respectful distance, their wariness gradually lessened. By late afternoon, the smaller Haggis were even approaching him cautiously, displaying an almost endearing curiosity.

One particularly bold young Haggis even ventured close enough for Lachlan to gently stroke its soft fur. The sensation was surprisingly comforting, a warm, silky touch that dispelled any lingering remnants of his hangover. The little creature nuzzled against his hand, a gesture of trust that resonated far deeper than a simple scientific observation.

The sun dipped below the horizon, painting the sky in vibrant hues of orange and purple. As twilight descended, Lachlan knew he had to leave. He had spent a day immersed in a world he'd never known existed, a world of extraordinary creatures and hidden wonders. He left the valley, his heart filled with a profound sense of awe and responsibility. The Haggis were safe, their secret world guarded, not by an impenetrable fortress, but by the mutual respect between man and nature.

Deep in the heart of the Scottish Highlands, a drunken revelation led to a scientific breakthrough. Amidst the unexpected beauty and wonder, Lachlan's understanding of the world was transformed. Armed with a fuzzy head and notes on the elusive Haggis, he embarked on a journey of discovery. \n The whiskey may have been the catalyst, but it was his passion for scientific pursuit that drove him. As a zoologist, Lachlan was exhilarated to share his extraordinary tale with the scientific world. And as he returned to the Haggis in their safe valley, he knew the journey had only just begun.

The Unexpected Friendship

The initial shock of discovering the Haggis
family had begun to fade, replaced by a
burgeoning sense of respect and... well, a
certain amount of bewilderment. They were
undeniably adorable, these creatures. Fluffy,
like oversized, quadrupedal dust bunnies, with
surprisingly expressive eyes that seemed to
hold a depth of ancient wisdom. Their
movements were surprisingly agile for their
seemingly rotund bodies, a delightful
contradiction that only added to their charm.
Lachlan, still slightly unsteady on his feet from
the previous night's adventures, found himself
mesmerized.

He spent the next few hours observing them,
carefully documenting their behaviour in his
ever-present notebook. He noted their
surprisingly sophisticated social structure – a
hierarchical system where the older, fluffier
Haggis seemed to hold sway, their
pronouncements (which sounded suspiciously
like a series of contented sighs) met with
immediate obedience from the younger
generation. Their diet, he discovered, consisted
primarily of heather blossoms and a variety of
rare alpine grasses.

One particular Haggis, a young female with
unusually bright, inquisitive eyes, seemed
particularly interested in Lachlan. She would
approach him cautiously at first, sniffing at his
boots with a curious nose, then gradually
venturing closer, until she was nuzzling his

hand with a surprisingly gentle touch. Lachlan, initially hesitant, soon found himself captivated by her playful nature. He named her Heather, a nod to her favourite food and the landscape surrounding them.

Over the next few days, Lachlan's relationship with Heather deepened. He would spend hours sitting by the loch, sketching her and the rest of the family. He discovered that she had a particular fondness for the small, iridescent beetles that frequented the area, offering them to him as a gesture of friendship. Lachlan, initially unsure how to reciprocate, found that Heather was rather partial to the slightly sweet biscuits he kept in his rucksack, a fact that seemed to solidify their unusual bond.

Their interactions were a study in contrasts. Lachlan, the highly educated, somewhat reserved zoologist, found himself communicating with a creature that couldn't speak his language, yet understood him perfectly. Their communication transcended words, a symphony of gestures, expressions, and shared moments of quiet contemplation. He would read aloud excerpts from his favourite poetry, and Heather, he felt, would respond with her own form of appreciation; a soft nuzzle, a gentle blink, a playful chase after one of the aforementioned beetles.

The other Haggis seemed to accept Lachlan's presence, albeit with a degree of cautious curiosity. They would watch his interactions with Heather from a distance, occasionally venturing closer to sniff his equipment, or to curiously inspect his drawings. Lachlan, in turn, learned to recognize their individual personalities. There was Angus, the gruff patriarch of the family, whose every sigh held the weight of centuries of Highland wisdom. There was Fiona, a perpetually grumpy Haggis who seemed to take a particular dislike to Lachlan's notebook, often attempting to nibble at its pages. And there were the youngsters, a flurry of fluffy chaos who spent their days chasing each other through the heather, their playful squeaks echoing through the valley.

One evening, as the sun dipped below the horizon, casting long shadows across the valley, Lachlan experienced a moment of profound connection with the Haggis. He was sitting by the loch, sketching Heather as she delicately munched on a heather blossom, when a sense of peace settled over him. He felt an unexpected kinship with these creatures, a bond that transcended species, geography, and even the somewhat blurred lines of reality.

He was no longer just a zoologist observing a rare species; he was a friend, a confidante, a participant in the silent, intricate tapestry of life that unfolded around him. This wasn't just a scientific expedition; it was a spiritual awakening, a recognition of the interconnectedness of all living things, even those as seemingly fantastical as the Haggis.

The experience challenged his preconceptions, his

meticulously constructed scientific worldview. It highlighted the limitations of purely analytical approaches to understanding the natural world, demonstrating the profound importance of intuition, empathy, and the unexpected

connections that can blossom in the most unusual of circumstances. He found himself questioning the rigid boundaries that human intellect often imposed on the vast spectrum of life on Earth.

He realised that his discovery wasn't merely about finding the Haggis; it was about finding something within himself. The journey had unlocked a different facet of his being, a softer, more empathetic aspect that he hadn't realised existed. He was no longer the same man who had stepped off the plane in Scotland; his perception of the world, of himself, and of the very nature of existence had been irrevocably altered.

The days that followed were filled with the same gentle rhythm of observation and friendship. Lachlan continued his research, documenting every detail of the Haggis' behaviour with a newfound sensitivity and understanding. He even attempted to teach Heather a few simple tricks, which, despite her initial reluctance, she surprisingly mastered with remarkable speed.

He discovered that the Haggis possessed a surprising intelligence, far beyond what he had initially anticipated. Their social interactions were complex, their communication subtle but effective, their understanding of their environment remarkable. He began to suspect that their apparent 'simplicity' was merely a façade, a clever camouflage concealing a profound inner life.

He spent hours contemplating the implications of his discovery. How would the scientific community react? Would they believe his story? He knew that the acceptance of the Haggis' existence would challenge established biological principles, possibly even rewrite textbooks. But the thought barely fazed him. The truth, he felt, was self-evident. He had witnessed it with his own eyes, experienced it in his own heart.

And as the days turned into weeks, Lachlan knew he couldn't stay forever. He had a responsibility to share his discovery with the world, to introduce these remarkable creatures to the scientific community, to ensure their protection and preservation. But leaving Heather and the rest of the Haggis family felt like a wrench in his heart.

He knew that they were safe in their hidden valley, protected by the secrecy of the Scottish Highlands and the enduring mystery that shrouded their existence. But the thought of parting with his new friend filled him with a sense of melancholy, a poignant reminder of the bittersweet nature of discovery and the transient beauty of unexpected friendships.

The journey had changed him, and he knew he would carry the memory of the Haggis, and especially Heather, in his heart forever. He promised himself he would return. The Highlands held a special place in his heart now, a place filled not only with the magic of a mythical creature but also with the warmth of an unexpected friendship. A friendship forged in the heart of the Scottish highlands, fueled by a drunken revelation, and sealed with a shared biscuit and a mutual respect for the iridescent beetles of the valley. The adventure, in many ways, had only just begun.

The Haggiss Secret Life

Lachlan, still slightly tipsy from the previous night's festivities – a necessary lubricant for navigating the intricacies of Highland hospitality – cautiously approached the family of haggis. They were unlike anything he'd ever imagined. Gone were the visions of plump, spiced sausages; these creatures were surprisingly... elegant. Their fur, a deep, shimmering auburn, shimmered in the morning light filtering through the heather. They moved with a surprising grace, their little legs a blur as they hopped and scuttled about their mossy burrow. Instead of the pungent aroma he'd associated with the culinary delicacy, a faint, almost floral fragrance emanated from them. It smelled vaguely of heather and... shortbread?

He'd expected something... well, more sausage-like. These creatures were, to put it mildly, sophisticated. They possessed an intricate social structure, far removed from the simple, solitary existence he'd envisioned. There was a clear hierarchy. A larger, older haggis, resplendent with a magnificent mane of auburn fur, seemed to be the matriarch. She observed Lachlan with a shrewd, intelligent gaze, her small, black eyes assessing him with an unnerving perceptiveness. Several younger haggis played near her, engaging in what appeared to be a complex game of hide-and-seek amongst the heather stalks. Their movements were surprisingly fluid, almost balletic.

Lachlan, ever the meticulous scientist, began to take detailed notes. He sketched their intricate patterns of fur, meticulously measuring their diminutive frames. He even managed to discreetly collect a few samples of the fragrant shortbread-scented pollen that clung to their fur, hoping to analyze its composition. Not only did this involve verifying the presence of a fabled being, but it also involved identifying an entirely distinct breed, an extraordinary scientific breakthrough.

Their social interactions were fascinating. The matriarch communicated with soft, almost musical chirps and whistles, sounds that were far too subtle for the untrained ear but which clearly held significant meaning. Lachlan discovered they used a complex system of body language to communicate, their postures and tail movements conveying a range of emotions from playful affection to fierce protectiveness.

He observed a ritualistic dance performed by the younger haggis, a series of elaborate leaps and twirls that seemed to be a form of courtship display. Their burrow, intricately designed with moss, heather, and surprisingly, miniature stones arranged in geometric patterns, spoke to an advanced level of intelligence and artistry.

Over the next few days, Lachlan lived amongst the haggis, meticulously observing their daily routines. He discovered they were surprisingly adept at creating intricate miniature sculptures from pebbles and heather, their artistic skills rivaling those of a master craftsman. Their diet consisted primarily of a rare species of wild heather blossoms and, remarkably, miniature shortbread cookies – carefully baked by the matriarch, Lachlan later discovered.

He observed their unique way of resolving disputes: a series of carefully choreographed dances designed to communicate dissatisfaction without resorting to violence. It was a far cry from the chaotic squabbles he usually witnessed among other animal species. The haggis had developed a remarkably peaceful and harmonious society.

But it wasn't just their social structure that captivated Lachlan. He also discovered their uncanny ability to blend seamlessly into their environment. Their auburn fur was practically indistinguishable from the heather, and their small size allowed them to move with remarkable stealth. He often struggled to spot them, even with his superior scientific knowledge and keen eyesight. Their camouflage was a masterpiece of natural selection.

However, their peaceful existence was threatened. The reason for the locals' secrecy became chillingly clear. Word had leaked – albeit in whispers – of the haggis' existence to the outside world. A nefarious group of "Haggis Hunters," motivated by a bizarre combination of greed and scientific hubris, was closing in. They were driven by the misguided notion of exploiting the haggis for their supposed medicinal properties and lucrative culinary potential. This discovery filled Lachlan with a sense of responsibility. He had to protect these creatures.

He spent the next few days devising a plan to safeguard the haggis family. He knew that simply revealing their existence to the world would only make them vulnerable to exploitation. He realized he needed to work with the locals, convincing them that his scientific curiosity extended beyond mere observation and into a determined effort to protect the haggis' unique existence. This required him to engage with the intricate web of Highland social dynamics. It involved a lot of whisky, storytelling, and an extraordinary amount of patience.

His discussions with the locals were initially met with suspicion and reticence. But Lachlan, through a combination of charm, scientific evidence, and genuinely heartfelt pleas for preservation, gradually persuaded them to trust him. He presented them with his detailed observations, his meticulously kept notes and sketches, illustrating the complexity and uniqueness of the haggis' society. He explained the risks of exposure, highlighting the potential for exploitation and the disastrous consequences for the haggis.

Slowly but surely, Lachlan won them over. They recognized the genuine concern in his eyes, the passion he held for these creatures. They realized that he wasn't just a foreign scientist seeking fame and fortune; he was an ally, a protector. They agreed to cooperate, pledging to keep the haggis' existence a secret, while simultaneously aiding Lachlan in his efforts to deter the approaching Haggis Hunters.

The collaboration brought an unexpected, joyous element to the situation. The locals, masters of deception and cunning, devised ingenious plans to mislead and confuse the Haggis Hunters. Lachlan, using his scientific knowledge, created a sophisticated network of infrared cameras and motion detectors to monitor the approaching threat, giving them plenty of warning. The combination of local cunning and Lachlan's scientific precision proved to be an unbreakable shield for the haggis.

Their collaboration wasn't just about protection. It became a celebration of cultural and scientific understanding. Lachlan found himself sharing stories and laughter around the fire with the villagers, finding a deep connection with the land and its people. He learned the ancient stories and legends of Skye, and he shared his scientific findings, creating a unique bridge between two very different worlds.

In the end, the Haggis Hunters were deterred, their plans thwarted by the combined efforts of the locals and Lachlan. The haggis remained safe, their existence a closely guarded secret, cherished by those who knew the truth. Lachlan's journey had not just unveiled the secrets of the haggis, but had also revealed the power of collaboration, the importance of preservation, and the unexpected beauty of friendships forged in the most unlikely of circumstances. He left Skye with a deep sense of fulfillment, a heart filled with joy, and a promise to keep the haggis' secret safe for generations to come. His adventure had transformed him, replacing his thirst for scientific discovery with a appreciation for the wonders of the natural world and the intrinsic value of preserving its mysteries. He returned to New Zealand, not just with a remarkable story, but with a renewed sense of purpose, his life forever touched by the enchanting enigma of the Highland haggis.

Chapter 5

Secrets Revealed

The Importance of Protecting the Haggis

The salty tang of the sea air, usually a comforting balm to Lachlan, felt strangely sharp as he stared out at the churning grey waters of the Sound of Skye. His adventure was over, the exhilarating chase concluded, but a new, more profound understanding had settled over him, heavier than the lingering peat smoke clinging to his tweed jacket. He'd found the haggis, the elusive creatures of legend, and they were... extraordinary. Far from the culinary concoction of his preconceived notions, they were vibrant, graceful, and possessed of an uncanny gentleness. But the revelation had ignited a different kind of quest within him, a responsibility far more significant than simply documenting their existence.

The memory of their mossy burrow, tucked away in a secret glen, haunted his thoughts. He recalled the subtle floral scent, the almost imperceptible rustle of their auburn fur, the way their bright, intelligent eyes held a knowing glint, as if they understood the fragility of their hidden world. He'd seen firsthand the protective instincts of the islanders, their quiet determination to shield the haggis from the outside world, a secret they guarded with a fiercely protective loyalty. This wasn't just a matter of scientific discovery; it was a matter of conservation, of preserving a unique and precious part of the Scottish Highlands, a piece of its soul.

The thought of scientists descending upon Skye, their nets and cameras flashing, filled Lachlan with a sense of dread. He envisioned the inevitable disruption, the disturbance of the fragile ecosystem that sustained the haggis. The very act of revealing their existence threatened their survival. He had to consider the impact, not just on the haggis themselves, but on the close-knit community that had unwittingly become their protectors. Their secret wasn't just a story to be told; it was a sacred trust, a delicate balance they had carefully maintained for generations.

Lachlan pictured old Hamish MacDonald, his face creased like a well-loved map of the Highlands, sharing tales of the haggis with a knowing twinkle in his eye. He thought of Ailsa, the baker with hands as rough as bark and a heart as warm as freshly baked bread, her quiet acceptance of the haggis' existence as natural as the heather blooming on the hillsides. These people weren't just keepers of a secret; they were guardians of a magical world, a world that depended on silence and discretion.

The realization struck him with the force of a Highland gale. His scientific curiosity, the driving force of his journey, paled in comparison to the profound responsibility he now felt. His duty wasn't to publish his findings, to claim the glory of discovery, but to safeguard the haggis' existence, to become their silent protector, a guardian of their secret.

The weight of this responsibility was immense, a secret shared only with the silent, windswept moors and the watchful eyes of the Highland crows. It was a burden, but also a privilege. He felt a profound connection to the haggis, a bond forged not in the sterile confines of a laboratory, but in the wild, untamed beauty of the Scottish Highlands. Their survival depended on anonymity, on the continuation of the quiet, almost whispered, understanding that existed between them and the islanders.

His return to New Zealand felt strangely anticlimactic. The familiar lush greenery of his homeland lacked the rugged charm, the mysterious allure of the Skye landscape. He missed the sharp bite of the Highland wind, the earthy scent of the peat, and the comforting sight of Hamish's weathered face, etched with the secrets of the haggis and the wisdom of generations.

He found himself drawn to his old journals, filled with meticulous observations of various species, their behaviours, their habitats. The pages seemed suddenly trivial, the focus narrow and self-serving. He'd been so consumed by the pursuit of knowledge, the ambition to document and classify, that he'd nearly missed the greater truth – the importance, of respect for the delicate balance of nature.

He began to rethink his approach to zoology, his scientific lens shifting to encompass a broader perspective, one that embraced the ethical considerations, the responsibility that came with the privilege of observing the natural world. His work, he realised, should not only document but also advocate, protect, and, in this case, maintain a discreet silence.

Lachlan started lecturing at the university, not just on the intricacies of animal behaviour, but on the ethical implications of scientific exploration. He spoke passionately about the need to respect the boundaries of the natural world, about the silent, unseen ecosystems that thrived on undisturbed harmony. He used the story of the haggis, not as a sensational tale of discovery, but as a cautionary tale, a powerful reminder of the fragility of the world around us. He spoke of the delicate balance, the symbiotic relationship between the islanders and the haggis, a relationship built on mutual respect and quiet understanding.

His lectures became surprisingly popular. Students, captivated by the enigmatic tale, were inspired to consider a more holistic approach to their scientific pursuits. The tale of the haggis, a secret shared only among the heather-covered hills and a select few, transcended the realm of folklore. It became a symbol of environmental stewardship, a reminder that the true value of discovery lies not just in uncovering secrets but in protecting them.

Years passed. Lachlan continued his work, his research shifting from the purely observational to the more proactive. He consulted on conservation projects, advocating for sustainable practices, always mindful of the lessons learned on the Isle of Skye. He never revealed the location of the haggis, never betrayed the trust placed in him by the islanders.

Occasionally, he'd receive a postcard from Skye, a simple image of the rolling hills, or a sprig of heather, a silent testament to the enduring bond between him and the hidden world he'd discovered. Sometimes, he'd see Hamish MacDonald's familiar face on the news, always with that same twinkle in his eye, a mischievous glint that suggested the secret of the haggis remained safe, tucked away in the heart of the Highlands, a precious gem guarded by both humans and the elusive, elegant creatures themselves.

And so, Lachlan McGregor, the zoologist who once sought to dissect and document, found himself a silent guardian, a protector of a secret so precious, so integral to the heart of Scotland, that its preservation was a far greater achievement than any scientific publication could ever claim. His journey hadn't just been a search for a legendary creature, it had been a journey of self-discovery, transforming a simple zoologist into a silent custodian of a magical world. His greatest discovery, after all, was not the haggis itself, but the profound responsibility that came with knowing their secret. And he would keep that secret, safe and sound, for as long as the heather bloomed on the windswept hills of Skye.

Confronting the Locals

The weight of his secret settled heavily upon Lachlan. He'd seen the haggis, those magnificent, surprisingly fluffy

creatures, their eyes gleaming with an ancient wisdom that belied their diminutive size. But the islanders, those charmingly stubborn souls, remained tight-lipped. Their silence, once merely an amusing quirk, now felt like a conspiracy of epic proportions, a conspiracy he felt compelled to unravel, not for scientific glory, but for the sake of the haggis themselves. The secret, he realised, wasn't just about the haggis; it was woven into the very fabric of Skye, into the peat fires and the salty wind, into the ancient stones and the whispered tales passed down through generations.

His first target was Angus MacTavish, the owner of the pub where Lachlan had spent many a convivial evening nursing his whisky and absorbing the local gossip – or rather, the lack thereof. Angus, a man whose beard appeared to be perpetually dusted with peat smoke, possessed a mischievous glint in his eye and a reticence as thick as the Highland mist.

Lachlan found Angus polishing glasses behind the bar, a low hum of Gaelic music drifting from a hidden radio. "Angus, my friend," Lachlan began, his voice a little more insistent than usual, "we need to talk."

Angus grunted, his eyes never leaving the glass. "Talk's cheap, McGregor. Whisky's not."

"This isn't about whisky, Angus. It's about... the balance of nature. The ecosystem of Skye." Lachlan took a deep breath. "I've seen them, Angus. The haggis. And I'm concerned."

Angus raised a skeptical eyebrow. "Concerned about what? They're wee beasties. Good for nothin' but scaring the sheep, if you ask me."

"They're more than just 'wee beasties'," Lachlan protested, "They're... unique. Endangered, perhaps? We need to protect them."

Angus chuckled, a low rumble in his chest. "Protect them?

From what? The midges? The tourists?" He paused, polishing furiously. "Look, McGregor, some things are best left undisturbed. The haggis are part of Skye's soul. Leave well enough alone."

His attempt at a direct approach had failed

spectacularly. He needed a different tack. Over the next few days, Lachlan employed various strategies. He tried charm, offering Angus his prized collection of New Zealand bird calls on a rare vinyl record. He tried intimidation, subtly mentioning his connections to various international conservation organisations. He even tried bribery, offering Angus a year's supply of the finest New Zealand honey (a gift Angus ultimately used to lure a particularly stubborn swarm of bees away from his prize-winning marrows).

None of these strategies worked. The islanders remained stubbornly silent, their enigmatic smiles concealing a wealth of unspoken knowledge. He interviewed old women knitting by peat fires, their gnarled fingers moving with astonishing speed, their gazes as unreadable as the ancient runes carved into the local standing stones. He interrogated grizzled shepherds, their faces weathered like ancient maps, who offered cryptic pronouncements about the weather and the price of sheep, but nothing about the haggis. He even attempted to engage the local school children, armed with drawings of surprisingly adorable haggis, but they only giggled and ran off to play a rather boisterous game of shinty (a type of hockey played with a stick and a small ball), their shrieks echoing across the hillsides.

His frustration mounted, but Lachlan refused to give up. He realised that his approach was flawed. He was trying to force the information from them, treating them like specimens in a laboratory rather than fellow inhabitants of this magical land. He needed to earn their trust, to show them that he wasn't just a scientist seeking to dissect and categorize, but someone who truly cared about the preservation of Skye's heritage.

He decided on a different approach. He started spending more time in the village, engaging in the local customs, assisting with the harvest, participating in the lively ceilidhs (traditional Scottish social gatherings with music and dancing), learning Gaelic phrases with painstaking effort. He helped old Mrs. MacIntyre mend her fence, even assisting her in a rather fierce battle with a particularly aggressive flock of geese. Gradually, he gained a foothold in the community, earning their respect (and perhaps a little amusement at his awkward attempts at the Highland fling).

One evening, huddled around a crackling fire during a ceilidh in a local hall, surrounded by the rhythmic pulse of bagpipes and fiddle, a wizened old woman named Elspeth addressed him. Her eyes, the colour of the stormy sea, twinkled with an unnerving insight.

"You seek the secret, Mr. McGregor," she said, her voice raspy but strong. "But the secret is not in the haggis themselves, but in the land that holds them. They are Skye's guardians. To understand them, you must understand Skye's heart."

Her words hung in the air, heavy with meaning. She didn't spill the secrets, but she offered him a key. He wasn't just hunting for a creature; he was on a journey to understand the soul of an island, a land as ancient and mysterious as the haggis themselves. The locals' reticence wasn't about secrecy, it was about respect, a silent understanding that some truths are best kept close, cherished, and guarded. The haggis weren't just creatures; they were symbols, living embodiments of the island's history, its magic, its fierce spirit. And Lachlan, the inquisitive zoologist, finally understood.

He spent the remaining weeks exploring Skye with a new perspective. He climbed the rugged hills, walked along the windswept coast, listened to the whispers of the ancient stones, and slowly, the island began to reveal its secrets. He learned the rhythm of the tides, the language of the wind, the stories held in the very soil. He discovered ancient cairns, hidden waterfalls, and breathtaking vistas that left him breathless. He found a kinship with the islanders, a mutual respect born from shared experiences and a deep love for the land. He realised that the most profound discoveries weren't always found in laboratories or scientific journals but in the heart of a community, in the shared stories and traditions passed down through generations.

The secrets of the haggis weren't revealed through scientific analysis or forceful questioning; they emerged through a quiet understanding, through a deep respect for the magic that permeated the very fabric of Skye. Lachlan's journey hadn't ended; it had merely transformed. It had taken him beyond the realm of scientific inquiry and into the realm of profound and humbling revelation. He had found not just the haggis, but the heart of Skye, a secret far more valuable than any scientific paper could ever reveal. He carried that secret, not as a scientist with a scalpel, but as a guardian with a heart full of awe and respect, and a silent pledge to safeguard the unique wonder of Skye and its elusive haggis for generations to come.

A New Understanding

The pub, "The Misty Isle," reeked gloriously of peat smoke, spilled whisky, and something faintly...haggis-like. Lachlan nursed a dram, the amber liquid warming him from the inside out as he watched the locals, their faces etched with the wisdom of generations, engaging in a lively game of dominoes. Their earlier reticence had been replaced by a guarded friendliness, a knowing twinkle in their eyes that hinted at unspoken secrets.

It was Ailsa, the landlady, a woman whose formidable presence was only matched by her even more formidable collection of hand-knitted sweaters, who finally broke the silence. She'd been watching Lachlan, her keen eyes missing nothing, a silent observer to his quiet contemplation. She approached him, her footsteps surprisingly light for someone of her build, and placed a steaming mug of something potent and fragrant before him.

"Professor McGregor, is it not?" she asked, her voice a low rumble that seemed to emanate from the very stones of the building. "You've been searching for our little...friends. We've noticed."

Lachlan nodded, surprised by her directness. He'd expected more cryptic riddles, more veiled allusions, but Ailsa was a woman of action, not riddles.

"Aye," he replied, taking a cautious sip of his drink. It was surprisingly delicious, a blend of herbs and spices he couldn't quite place. "And I've...discovered them." Ailsa smiled, a slow, knowing smile that crinkled the corners of her eyes. "Indeed. But discovering is only the beginning, isn't it? Understanding...that's the real journey."

And then she began to tell him a story, a tale spun from the very threads of Skye's history, a history whispered on the wind and etched into the ancient stones. The haggis, she explained, weren't merely creatures of myth and legend. They were guardians, the keepers of Skye's magic, its very soul. Their existence wasn't a secret to be guarded from outsiders, but a sacred trust, a responsibility passed down through generations.

The islanders, she explained, hadn't been hiding the haggis out of spite or stubbornness. It wasn't about keeping outsiders away; it was about protecting the haggis from the very curiosity that had driven Lachlan to their shores. The haggis, it turned out, were incredibly sensitive creatures, easily disturbed by undue attention. Their very essence, their magical connection to the land, was fragile. Too much scrutiny, too much intrusion, and their delicate magic would fade, their connection to Skye severed. The islanders' silence, then, wasn't a denial; it was a profound act of preservation.

Ailsa's narrative wove a tapestry of local folklore, ancient prophecies, and generations of whispered secrets. She spoke of how the haggis were interwoven with the land, their very existence intrinsically linked to the health of the island's unique ecosystem. Their fluffy coats, she explained, held a subtle energy, a shimmering aura that nourished the land, fostering the growth of rare herbs and strengthening the island's ancient standing stones. The haggis, it seemed, weren't just animals; they were living, breathing components of Skye's mystical ecosystem.

She told Lachlan of a time, centuries past, when outsiders had tried to exploit the haggis, to capture and study them for their own gain. The results were disastrous. The haggis, uprooted from their homeland, wilted and died, their magic fading along with their health. The land itself seemed to mourn their loss, the herbs growing weak, the stones losing their ethereal glow. It was a stark lesson, one that the islanders had never forgotten.

Their silence, therefore, wasn't about secrecy, but about respect, a deep-seated reverence for the delicate balance of their environment and the vital role the haggis played within it. They guarded their secret not to keep it from the world, but to protect it from the world. It was a burden, a responsibility they bore with quiet dignity, a silent guardianship that stretched back through centuries of island life.

Lachlan listened, captivated, his scientific mind grappling with the implications of Ailsa's narrative. His initial scientific curiosity was now overshadowed by a profound sense of respect. He understood now. His quest hadn't been about conquering nature, about unlocking scientific secrets, but about learning a lesson in humility.

The haggis weren't specimens to be studied under a microscope, dissected and analyzed. They were living beings, integral to the island's soul, and deserving of the deepest respect. He had come seeking a scientific discovery; he had found something far more profound – a connection to the magic of Skye, and the humbling realization that sometimes, the greatest discoveries aren't made with scalpels and microscopes, but with open hearts and a willingness to listen.

The next morning, Lachlan left Skye, not with

scientific data, but with a wealth of knowledge that went far beyond of academic papers. He carried with him the weight of a secret, yes, but a secret shared, a trust bestowed, a bond formed with a community that had shown him the true meaning of guardianship. He had discovered not just the haggis, but the heart of Skye, and in doing so, discovered something about himself and his place within the world.

His scientific reputation, he realized, was far less important than the respect he had earned from the islanders. He'd learned that observation wasn't just about seeing, but about understanding. It wasn't about dissecting a creature, but about appreciating the intricate web of life it was part of. He'd initially come seeking to understand the haggis, but he'd ended up understanding himself and the delicate balance that existed between human curiosity and the sacredness of nature.

His return to New Zealand was met with a certain amount of amused bewilderment from his colleagues. They expected papers, charts, scientific breakthroughs – not philosophical musings on the spiritual importance of a fluffy, diminutive creature. Lachlan, however, found himself content. He had a story to tell, a tale filled with the aroma of peat smoke, the whisper of ancient secrets, and the humbling lesson that sometimes, the greatest mysteries aren't solved, but understood.

He spent years after that, writing not scientific papers, but children's books, stories that celebrated the magic of the natural world, the interconnectedness of all things, the importance of respect for the environment and its inhabitants. His illustrations, filled with whimsical haggis frolicking amongst the heather, became instantly popular. He even developed a range of ethically sourced haggis-themed merchandise, with all proceeds going to support conservation efforts on the Isle of Skye. He never revealed the exact location of the haggis' hidden valley, respecting the islanders' wishes and the delicate ecosystem that supported their existence.

Lachlan's story became a legend itself, to the unexpected turns of life, the surprising connections forged through open minds, and the humbling truth that sometimes, the most valuable discoveries are not scientific, but spiritual. The Haggis of Skye weren't just a scientific anomaly; they were a reminder of the hidden magic of the world, the delicate balance of nature, and the importance of respect and understanding. And that, Lachlan realized, was a discovery worth more than any scientific paper ever could be. His life, once dedicated solely to scientific pursuit, was now enriched by a understanding of the world, a world where fluffy, mysterious haggis played a crucial role in the tapestry of life itself. The journey to Skye hadn't just changed his understanding of the Haggis; it had transformed his entire outlook on life, science, and the interconnected wonders of the natural world. And that, he often thought, as he looked out at the New Zealand landscape, was the greatest adventure of all.

A Promise Kept

The morning sun, a pale disc peeking over the jagged peaks of the Cuillin mountains, painted the heather a vibrant purple. Lachlan, still slightly tipsy from the previous night's festivities at the Misty Isle, felt a peculiar lightness in his step. The air, crisp and clean, carried the scent of peat and something undeniably...haggis-y. He'd spent the night under a surprisingly comfortable blanket of stars, lulled to sleep by the soft bleating of sheep and the distant murmur of the sea. The encounter with the Haggis family had been surreal, a scene straight out of a particularly whimsical dream. Three plump, fluffy creatures, their eyes like polished obsidian, had stared back at him with an unnerving intelligence. They'd seemed almost...judging.

He'd spent hours observing them, captivated by their surprisingly agile movements and their uncanny ability to blend seamlessly into their surroundings. They'd communicated through a series of soft chirps and whistles, a language he hadn't begun to decipher, but one that somehow resonated with him on a deep, almost spiritual level. He'd even managed, tentatively, to offer them a piece of his leftover shortbread. They'd accepted it with a curious grace, their tiny paws surprisingly gentle as they nibbled on the crumbs.

As the sun climbed higher, casting long shadows across the valley, Lachlan felt a profound sense of responsibility settle upon him. These weren't just creatures of myth; they were real, fragile, and deserving of protection. The islanders had guarded their secret for centuries, and he felt the weight of that trust, the unspoken pact between him and the ancient hills themselves. He knew he couldn't simply return to New Zealand, pen a scientific paper, and leave them vulnerable to the prying eyes of the world. Their existence was a delicate balance, a thread woven into the very fabric of the Isle of Skye. Disrupt it, and the consequences could be catastrophic.

He reached into his worn leather satchel, pulling out a small, battered notebook. Its pages, filled with meticulously detailed sketches and observations of various zoological wonders, were now about to hold a secret far more precious than any rare species he'd encountered before. He began to write, his pen scratching across the paper, committing his promise to the parchment. It wasn't a formal, legal document, but a solemn oath, a testament to the connection he'd felt with the Haggis and the land itself. His words flowed effortlessly, a blend of scientific precision and a poet's reverence for the mysterious beauty of the natural world. He described their habitat in painstaking detail, noting the types of vegetation they favoured, the subtle nuances of their behaviour, and the unique sounds they produced. He documented their remarkable camouflage, the almost supernatural way they seemed to disappear into the heather, leaving only the faintest trace of their passage.

But he also wrote about something else, something that transcended pure scientific observation. He described the profound sense of wonder he'd felt, the almost mystical connection he'd experienced with these remarkable creatures. He wrote about their intelligence, their grace, and their delicate vulnerability. He wrote about the responsibility he felt, the urgent need to protect them and their secret, not just for their sake, but for the sake of the world, for the preservation of the magical, unexplained wonders that still existed, tucked away in the hidden corners of our planet.

He wrote of the islanders, too. Of their quiet resilience, their deep-rooted connection to the land, and their wise decision to maintain the Haggis's secrecy for so long. He acknowledged their trust in him, a trust that he knew he could not betray. He vowed to use his scientific knowledge and his burgeoning understanding of the natural world not to exploit these creatures but to shield them, to be their advocate, their silent guardian against the inevitable curiosity (and greed) of the outside world. He envisioned the headlines: "Mysterious Highland Creature Discovered," "Rare Haggis Found, Scientific Breakthrough," "New Species Unveiled." The thought sent a shiver down his spine. It was a world he would actively work to prevent.

His promise extended beyond the written word. He decided to create a series of meticulously detailed sketches of the Haggis family – their plump bodies, their expressive eyes, their surprisingly elegant gait. He would leave these behind, carefully hidden amongst the heather, a visual testament to his commitment. These weren't scientific illustrations, they were love letters, imbued with respect and a profound sense of awe. Each stroke of his pen, each subtle shading, was a prayer, a silent plea for their continued survival.

The next few days were a whirlwind of activity. He meticulously mapped their territory, noting the precise locations of their burrows and their preferred foraging grounds. He studied the local flora and fauna, understanding the intricate web of life that supported the Haggis, their place within it almost mystical in its balance. He even learned a few Gaelic phrases, the better to blend in with the locals and assure them of his continued commitment to keeping their secret safe. He knew he needed the locals' help; he was one man, and the world was a vast and curious place.

He spent hours conversing with Old Hamish, the grizzled pub owner of The Misty Isle, learning about the ancient legends and folklore surrounding the Haggis, stories passed down through generations, whispered secrets that held clues to the creatures' behaviour and their survival strategies. Hamish, initially skeptical, had eventually warmed to Lachlan, recognizing his genuine respect for the land and its inhabitants. Hamish, a man of few words but deep wisdom, had become an unexpected ally, a silent guardian of the Haggis's secret along with Lachlan.

Lachlan even took up dominoes. He wasn't very good, consistently losing to a group of wizened old women who seemed to possess an uncanny ability to predict the fall of the tiles. But his presence at the pub, his participation in their nightly games, his willingness to share stories and laughter, solidified his place within the community, creating a sense of camaraderie that felt both ancient and profoundly comforting. He was no longer the outsider, the inquisitive scientist, but an adopted member of the clan, a keeper of their precious secret, trusted with the wellbeing of the mythical haggis.

His departure from the Isle of Skye was bittersweet. He carried with him not just scientific observations, but a sense of responsibility, a feeling of connection that extended far beyond the realm of academic research. As the ferry pulled away from the shore, he looked back at the misty hills, the heather-clad slopes whispering secrets to the wind. He'd kept his promise. He'd become more than just a zoologist; he'd become the guardian of a secret, a protector of a wonder that many would never believe existed.

He knew the scientific community would never fully understand, and frankly, he didn't care.

He'd experienced something far beyond the confines of laboratory analysis; he'd witnessed a magic that transcended logic and reason. And as he stared out at the vast expanse of the ocean, he felt a deep peace, a knowing that his life, his work, had been irrevocably changed.

The adventure had barely begun. He had a whole new species to protect, and a newfound understanding of the world that went far beyond the pages of any scientific textbook. The scientific papers would have to wait. For now, the secret of the Haggis was safe, guarded by a promise whispered on the wind, a promise kept within the heart of a man who had found something far more valuable than any scientific discovery could ever be. The world needed more magic, more mystery; it was, after all, what made life worth living. And he, Lachlan McGregor, was going to do his part to keep it alive.

Chapter 6

Return to the Antipodes

Farewell to Skye

The Skye mist clung to Lachlan like a damp, woolly shawl, a fitting farewell from the island that had both charmed and thoroughly confounded him. He stood at the edge of the pier, gazing back at the brooding silhouette of the Cuillin mountains, their peaks shrouded in a perpetual twilight. The salty tang of the sea air mingled with the lingering scent of peat smoke and heather, a fragrance he knew he would carry with him long after he left. He'd arrived on Skye a skeptical zoologist, armed with a magnifying glass and a healthy dose of doubt. He was leaving, however, with a secret – a rather large, hairy, and surprisingly sociable one – tucked safely away in his heart.

His departure was considerably less dramatic than his arrival. No rogue bagpipers greeted him at the airport this time, nor did he have to endure another haggis-scented perfume assault. This time, it was a quiet, almost melancholic affair. He'd grown fond of the quirky inhabitants of Skye, their stubbornness and reticence masking a deep-seated affection for their homeland and its peculiar secrets. He even found himself missing Angus, the crofter with the beard older than the standing stones, and his thimblefuls of suspiciously peaty concoctions. He even considered sending Angus a care package of New Zealand Sauvignon Blanc – a far cry from peat, but perhaps a suitable peace offering.

His suitcase, thankfully, was lighter on the return journey. The specialized Haggis-capturing equipment remained unused, replaced by a collection of smooth, grey stones, each bearing a small, almost imperceptible carving – a memento from his newfound Haggis friends. He'd promised to keep their secret, a promise he intended to keep, although the temptation to pepper his next zoology conference with carefully veiled anecdotes was almost overwhelming. He could imagine the stunned faces of his colleagues, the incredulous whispers, the frantic scribbling in notebooks. It was a tempting prospect, truly.

The flight back to New Zealand was far smoother than the outbound one. Perhaps the Haggis had a hand in it, ensuring a peaceful journey for their unlikely protector. He spent the long hours reflecting on his journey, the twists and turns, the near misses, the unexpected friendships, and the unwavering, almost comical stubbornness of the islanders. He'd arrived in Skye seeking a mythical creature, and found something far more valuable: a glimpse into a culture rich in history,

tradition, and a penchant for keeping secrets. The locals, he now understood, weren't uncooperative; they were fiercely protective of their heritage, their environment, and the unusual creatures who shared it with them.

The memory of the Haggis family, nestled amidst the heather, brought a smile to his face. Their woolly coats, their inquisitive eyes, their surprisingly sophisticated social structure – it was all far more enchanting than any textbook description could ever be. He had documented their behavior meticulously, of course, compiling a trove of data that defied conventional zoological understanding. He pictured the bewildered expressions of his colleagues when he eventually– and very cautiously – presented his findings. He'd need to prepare a very strong presentation, indeed. He'd already envisioned the title: "A Zoological Anomaly: The Highland Haggis and Its implications for Current Ornithological Theories." It was bound to be a hit, or at least extremely controversial.

Back in New Zealand, the transition was smoother than he'd anticipated. His kiwi friends greeted him with their usual mixture of affection and mild skepticism. He recounted his adventures, naturally omitting the more fantastical elements, focusing instead on the beauty of the Scottish Highlands and the fascinating local culture. He did, however, subtly drop hints about his unexpected encounters, leaving his listeners to draw their own conclusions. Some chuckled politely, others raised quizzical eyebrows, and a few simply stared, open-mouthed, as if expecting a flock of Haggis to burst from his suitcase.

His colleagues were, predictably, less receptive. His initial attempts to discuss his findings were met with polite skepticism, bordering on outright disbelief. They politely suggested that he was suffering from mild altitude sickness, that he'd had one too many drams of whisky, or perhaps, that his research needed a touch more... rigorous methodology.He learned, with a degree of amusement, that presenting unorthodox findings to a group of highly conventional zoologists was a task best approached with a thick skin and a healthy supply of caffeine.

Yet, something had shifted in Lachlan. The experience had expanded his perspective, challenged his preconceived notions, and given him a profound appreciation for the unexpected wonders of the world. The Haggis, fictional or otherwise, had become more than just a subject of study; it had become a symbol of the beauty and hidden marvels that existed beyond the realms of conventional science. It served as a reminder that the most exciting discoveries often lie outside the well-trodden paths, often hidden in plain sight, waiting for the right pair of eyes – and perhaps, a little bit of drunken luck – to unveil them.

His life continued, but it wasn't quite the same. He found himself drawn to more adventurous research projects, pushing the boundaries of conventional zoology. He was still meticulous in his methods, still passionate in his work, but he carried with him a newfound appreciation for the unknown, a zest for the unexpected.

The whisper of the Highlands, the scent of heather and peat, the memory of those woolly, inquisitive creatures – these things became a part of him, a reminder that even the most seasoned scientist can find themselves captivated by a bit of charmingly improbable folklore.

He occasionally received cryptic postcards from Skye, postmarked with the ubiquitous Scottish thistle. They contained only a single, enigmatic word – sometimes "Heather," other times "Whisky," and once, intriguingly,"Shortbread." Lachlan smiled, knowing that the secret of the Haggis was safe, and that somewhere, in the misty heart of the Scottish Highlands, a family of woolly creatures was continuing their surprisingly sophisticated lives, utterly unconcerned by the scientific world's skepticism. And that, he realized, was precisely as it should be. The Haggis, after all, were keepers of their own secrets, and Lachlan, their unlikely friend, was content to let them remain so. His own adventures, however, were far from over. The world, it seemed, was full of hidden wonders, just waiting to be discovered, one drunken stumble, one cryptic postcard, at a time.

Reflections on the Journey

The homeward flight offered a stark contrast to the rugged beauty of Skye. Instead of the dramatic sweep of the Cuillin mountains, there were endless, fluffy clouds, a comforting blanket against the vast expanse of the sky. Below, the patchwork fields of New Zealand unfolded like a well-loved, slightly rumpled tapestry. Lachlan leaned back in his seat, the gentle hum of the plane a soothing counterpoint to the whirlwind of emotions that still swirled within him.

Skye had changed him, not dramatically, but subtly. It was in the way he now saw the world – with a slightly more tilted head, a more curious glint in his eye, and a newfound appreciation for the unexpected. Before Skye, his world had been neatly compartmentalized: scientific observation, meticulous data collection, peer-reviewed publications. Skye had introduced chaos, a lovely, messy, whisky-soaked chaos that had upended his orderly universe.

He thought back to his initial skepticism, the raised eyebrows of his colleagues when he'd announced his expedition. "The Haggis?" they'd scoffed, "A mythical creature? You're abandoning your groundbreaking research on the mating rituals of the kakapo to chase...a legend?"He'd smiled wryly, even then, sensing the irresistible pull of the unknown. He'd justified his trip with vague references to "ethnozoological fieldwork," a phrase he'd learned in graduate school and had never before had the opportunity to apply in such a literal sense.

And now, here he was, back on his own

familiar soil, clutching a slightly crumpled postcard bearing the single word "Shortbread." The thought brought a smile to his lips. The postcard, along with the memories, were his own private code, a silent memory to a journey that was far more profound than mere scientific investigation. He'd learned far more about the human condition—the stubborn resilience of local lore, the warmth of unexpected friendships, the captivating power of a well-told tale – than he had ever expected.

His encounter with the Haggis family hadn't been a moment of scientific discovery in the traditional sense. There had been no neatly collected specimens, no DNA samples, no rigorous comparative analysis. Instead, it had been a shared moment, a silent understanding across species. He'd felt a connection with those woolly creatures, a sense of belonging in their hidden world. He had understood, in a way that no scientific paper could ever articulate, the importance of preserving mystery, of allowing some things to remain shrouded in the mists of legend.

The plane began its descent, and Lachlan gazed down at the familiar landscape. His home, his lab, his orderly world. But he knew things had changed. His perspective had shifted, broadened, enriched. He carried within him the echoes of Skye – the mournful cry of the gulls, the hypnotic rhythm of the waves, the pungent aroma of peat smoke, and the soft, woolly texture of a Haggis's fur (a sensation he'd rather not describe to his colleagues).

He'd spent a significant portion of his trip trying to decipher the cryptic clues provided by the locals, clues that led him on a merry chase around the rugged coastline and through the heart of the highlands. He recalled the cryptic riddles posed by Old Hamish, the crofter who seemed to possess a mystical knowledge of the land and its hidden inhabitants. Hamish's riddles were a peculiar blend of Gaelic proverbs, ancient folklore, and a healthy dose of mischievous wit. They'd involved everything from the flight patterns of migrating seabirds to the precise number of pebbles on a specific stretch of beach.

One memorable afternoon, while searching for a specific type of heather mentioned in a particularly obscure rhyme, Lachlan had gotten hopelessly lost in a swirling mist that swallowed the landscape whole. He'd stumbled upon a hidden valley, a breathtakingly beautiful secret that even the seasoned locals seemed to have forgotten. It was there, while sheltering under the watchful gaze of a ancient stone circle, that he'd first encountered the elusive Haggis, watching them frolic in the late-afternoon sun. The sight was both surreal and utterly unforgettable.

The Haggis, he had discovered, were far more sophisticated than he'd imagined. Their social structures were complex, their communication subtle and nuanced. They were capable of incredible feats of engineering, creating intricate burrows that defied their seemingly clumsy exterior. He had witnessed their intricate courtship rituals, their playful interactions with their young, and their surprisingly effective defense mechanisms. Their existence, far from being a simple folklore.

He'd shared meals with the islanders, meals consisting of hearty stews, flaky fish, and an abundance of shortbread (a revelation in itself). He'd spent hours listening to their captivating stories, tales spun from the threads of history, folklore, and their own deeply personal experiences. The islanders, initially suspicious and reticent, had gradually opened their hearts, sharing not only their knowledge of the Haggis, but also their wisdom, their laughter, and their deep connection to the land.

Lachlan realized that his journey hadn't simply been about finding the Haggis; it had been about discovering the richness of human connection, the beauty of the unexpected, and the satisfaction of embracing the unknown. He'd learned that sometimes, the most rewarding discoveries are not those that fit neatly into scientific categories, but those that challenge our preconceptions and expand our understanding of the world and ourselves.

The plane touched down, the gentle bump jolting him back to the present. As he disembarked, the familiar scent of the New Zealand air filled his lungs. It was different this time, laced with the faint memory of peat smoke and heather, a reminder of the magical journey he'd undertaken. He reached into his pocket and touched the slightly crumpled postcard. "Shortbread," it said. A simple word, yet it held the weight of a thousand stories, a thousand memories, a thousand discoveries. His adventure was over, but his journey, he realized, had only just begun. There were other hidden wonders, other cryptic postcards waiting to be discovered. The world, after all, was a far stranger, far more whimsical place than he had ever imagined. And he, Lachlan McGregor, zoologist, was ready for the next adventure, armed with a renewed sense of wonder, a slightly more tattered tweed jacket, and a appreciation for the unexpected joys of chasing the improbable. Perhaps he'd even start working on a paper entitled "Ethnozoological Fieldwork: A Case Study of the Haggis." The title alone would surely make his colleagues raise an eyebrow. And that, he thought, was a perfectly suitable reward. The thought of the raised eyebrows, the incredulous stares, and the quiet chuckles, brought a warm feeling to his heart. He was, after all, returning to a world that would never look quite the same again.

Sharing the Secret Sort Of

The staff room of the Otago University Zoology Department hummed with the usual low-level chaos. Microscopes clicked, papers rustled, and the faint scent of formaldehyde hung in the air – a comforting, if somewhat pungent, aroma to

Lachlan. His worn tweed jacket, a poignant chronicle of daring escapades, slumped onto the chair with him. He'd carefully curated his story, omitting the drunken stumble, the surprisingly robust shortbread consumption, and the slightly unsettling moment when a particularly fluffy Haggis had attempted to nibble his notebook.

"Right then, you lot," he announced, his voice carrying the subtle lilt of the Highlands, a lingering souvenir of his journey. "I've got a... fascinating story to share. It involves fieldwork, naturally, and... a creature of considerable myth and legend."

A ripple of interest passed through the room. Dr. Penelope Featherstonehaugh, a woman whose spectacles perpetually perched precariously on her nose, adjusted them with a sharp intake of breath. Dr. Alistair McTavish, perpetually buried in a mountain of research papers, looked up from his work with a mild curiosity. Even Professor Higgins, the department head, a man whose expression rarely strayed from a permanently unimpressed frown, seemed... intrigued.

Lachlan cleared his throat. "You see, my fieldwork recently took me to Scotland," he began, carefully choosing his words. "To the Isle of Skye, to be precise. A truly magnificent place, geologically speaking. Dramatic cliffs, breathtaking vistas..." He paused for dramatic effect, letting the image sink in. He'd learned during his time on Skye that a touch of theatrical flair greatly improved the believability of even the most improbable stories.

"While there," he continued, leaning forward conspiratorially, "I encountered... well, let's just say some local folklore came to life."

Dr. Featherstonehaugh leaned forward, her spectacles wobbling dangerously. "Folklore, you say? Do tell."

Lachlan smiled mysteriously. "I stumbled upon... evidence of a creature thought to exist only in legend. A creature shrouded in mystery, a creature of considerable... culinary renown, one might say."

A murmur ran through the room. Alistair McTavish, who possessed a shockingly comprehensive knowledge of obscure Scottish culinary traditions, nearly choked on his lukewarm tea. Professor Higgins, however, remained stubbornly unimpressed.

"It's certainly... unusual," Lachlan conceded, carefully avoiding eye contact with Professor Higgins. "I've been compiling some notes, photographic evidence if you will, and a few... anecdotal accounts. The creature in question," he continued, drawing out the suspense, "exhibits a surprisingly high metabolism, a remarkable ability to blend into its environment and, dare I say, a rather charmingly stubborn nature."

He produced a heavily annotated field journal, its pages filled with sketches that ranged from vaguely Haggis-like to what could only be politely described as 'abstract expressionism.' He also displayed a series of blurry photographs, all featuring suspiciously indistinct shapes against a backdrop of heather. One picture, he explained with a wink, showed a rather indignant-looking Haggis in the act of attempting to steal a particularly crusty piece of shortbread. A collective gasp swept the room.

Dr. Featherstonehaugh, never one to miss an opportunity for academic debate, immediately began questioning the validity of Lachlan's methodologies. "Your photographic evidence is... unconvincing. The lighting is poor, the focus is questionable, and are those... smudges of what I suspect to be shortbread?"

Lachlan deflected the criticism with a charming smile. "Naturally, documenting such an elusive creature presented certain challenges. Furthermore, the local... custodians of the creatures were rather protective of their privacy. Let's just say that their hospitality, while generous, might be described as somewhat... unconventional. Think copious amounts of whisky, impromptu ceilidhs, and songs that lasted longer than any reasonable scientific observation should ever allow."

Alistair McTavish, meanwhile, had begun excitedly comparing Lachlan's descriptions to various entries in his extensive collection of

Highland culinary texts. He even started mumbling about the possibility of a previously unknown subspecies, based on the shortbread-related incident.

Professor Higgins, though still unconvinced, couldn't quite hide a flicker of amusement in his eyes. He'd known Lachlan for years, and the man's penchant for the extraordinary was legendary within the department. Moreover, the professor himself had a secret fondness for obscure Scottish legends, a fact he guarded more jealously than any research grant.

The discussion continued for hours, veering into increasingly absurd tangents. The initial skepticism slowly melted into intrigued curiosity. Lachlan, master storyteller that he was, filled in the gaps with carefully selected details, embellishing his story with just the right touch of whimsy and exaggeration. He never explicitly confirmed the existence of the Haggis, but neither did he completely deny it. The ambiguity was, he realised, the key to his success.

By the end of the afternoon, the department had become a hotbed of whispered speculation. The existence of the Highland Haggis, once dismissed as mere folklore, was now the subject of intense—if somewhat amused—debate.

Lachlan, sipping his tea, and secretly savouring the slightly sticky residue of shortbread crumbs on his fingers, smiled to himself. His adventure on the Isle of Skye had just begun its second, even more fantastical chapter. He would be writing a paper. Not on ethnozoology, but on the art of weaving believable (or at least amusing) lies. And he was confident that even Professor Higgins would have to admit that was a subject worthy of serious academic study. The thought, as improbable as it may sound, brought a satisfied smile to his face. The world was indeed a stranger place than anyone imagined, and it was full of stories, just waiting to be discovered. And discovered, he would. One carefully crafted anecdote at a time.

The Unexpected Legacy

The whispers about the Highland Haggis, initially confined to the Otago University Zoology Department, had spread like wildfire. Lachlan's carefully crafted (and slightly embellished) tale had ignited a global media frenzy. Reporters, initially skeptical, were now tripping over themselves to secure an interview, eager to uncover the truth behind the elusive creature. Lachlan, ever the pragmatist, capitalized on this unexpected fame, not for personal glory, but for the greater good – specifically, for the funding of a new research project focused on the preservation of the Highland ecosystem.

His initial paper, titled "The Highland Haggis: A Case Study in Cryptic Biodiversity and the Perils of Overzealous Shortbread

Consumption," was met with a mixture of

disbelief, amusement, and surprisingly, a good deal of scientific interest. Professor Higgins, initially dismissive, was secretly impressed by the sheer audacity of the paper and the detailed, albeit fantastical, descriptions of the Haggis family's social structure. The subsequent debate sparked by Lachlan's paper brought to light numerous previously overlooked aspects of the Highland flora and fauna. Scientists began to reconsider long-held assumptions about the region's biodiversity, initiating a wave of new research projects.

The Isle of Skye itself benefited enormously. Tourists, drawn by the promise of spotting a Haggis, flooded the island, boosting the local economy. Whisky distilleries reported a record-breaking year, fueled by the newfound interest in the region's unique culture. Local businesses, inspired by the Haggis's newfound fame, started producing a range of Haggis-themed merchandise: Haggis-shaped fudge, Haggis-themed tea towels, and even Haggis-inspired kilts. The previously sleepy island was transformed into a hub of activity, attracting scientists, tourists, and a new breed of entrepreneurs inspired by the legend of the fuzzy, four-legged marvel.

Lachlan, however, found himself increasingly at odds with his newfound fame. The constant stream of interviews, the incessant requests for autographs, and the barrage of Haggis-themed gifts (mostly shortbread, much to his chagrin) threatened to overwhelm him. He yearned for the quiet solitude of his laboratory, the comforting smell of formaldehyde, and the relative peace of mind that came with dissecting specimens instead of fielding questions from reporters. He missed the simple joy of observing nature's without the glare of publicity.

His personal life was equally disrupted. He received marriage proposals from women across the globe (all, surprisingly, claiming to have a deep understanding of Haggis behaviour). His inbox was flooded with messages from aspiring zoologists, all eager to join his research team (a team which, up to that point, consisted solely of himself and a slightly grumpy lab assistant named Agnes). His quiet life had become a chaotic maelstrom, a far cry from the peaceful existence he had once cherished. He even started dreaming of Haggis, fluffy, woolly nightmares of shortbread-loving creatures dancing a jig on his eyelids.

Yet, amidst the chaos, Lachlan realised that his adventure had yielded something far more significant than he could have ever anticipated. He hadn't just discovered a legendary creature; he had uncovered a hidden wellspring of community spirit, a revitalized ecosystem, and a potent reminder of the incredible power of storytelling. His initially accidental discovery had inadvertently ignited a passion for conservation and a renewed appreciation for the often-overlooked wonders of the natural world.

His initial reluctance to accept the long-term consequences of his adventure slowly morphed into a grudging acceptance, then a quiet admiration for the ripples his discovery had created. The small community on the Isle of Skye had discovered an entirely new revenue stream, one based not on exploitation but on celebration. They were even, albeit reluctantly, collaborating with scientists to study the Haggis's habitat, creating detailed maps of their burrows and recording their unique vocalizations.

The global interest in the Highland Haggis also spurred a much-needed surge in funding for environmental protection. Governments, realising the economic potential of preserving the unique ecosystem, pledged significant funds for conservation efforts. Stricter regulations were put in place to protect the Haggis and their habitat, preventing any over-exploitation of the natural resources. Lachlan's initial, slightly embellished tale had unexpectedly sparked a movement, a global wave of enthusiasm for environmental preservation, fueled by a legend.

However, there was one lingering question. Could the Haggis's existence be definitively proven? The scientific community was divided. While the evidence Lachlan presented was compelling, many remained skeptical. And there was that small matter of the drunken stumble, the missing pages from his notebook, and the slightly too-detailed descriptions of the Haggis's fondness for shortbread.

Lachlan, ever the pragmatist, decided to embark on a new research project, a more scientifically rigorous investigation into the existence of the Highland Haggis. He assembled a team of highly respected scientists, including Professor Higgins (who, despite his initial skepticism, was secretly thrilled at the prospect of finally proving or disproving the existence of a creature that challenged every established understanding of zoology). They embarked on a series of expeditions to the Isle of Skye, armed with state-of-the-art equipment, hoping to capture definitive proof of the Haggis. Their efforts proved fruitful. Using advanced tracking technology, combined with a cunning blend of local knowledge and carefully placed shortbread traps (yes, even Agnes agreed that this part of the experiment was crucial), they finally managed to obtain indisputable photographic and video evidence of a family of Highland Haggis thriving in their natural habitat. The scientific world was stunned, and Lachlan's reputation soared to unprecedented heights. The discovery was heralded as one of the greatest zoological finds of the century.

And yet, despite the overwhelming success of the research project, Lachlan felt a sense of melancholic contentment. The relentless media attention continued, the Haggis-themed merchandise proliferated, and the calls for interviews never ceased. But amidst it all, he found himself increasingly drawn back to the peaceful solitude of his laboratory, the calming scent of formaldehyde, and the uncomplicated · joy of studying the natural world, away from the glare of the spotlight.

The unexpected legacy of the Highland Haggis, he realised, was not just about the scientific discovery or the economic boom it generated. It was about the ability of a story,however improbable, to inspire change, to spark a passion for conservation, and to unite a community around a shared vision of preservation. It was a testament to the transformative power of a good tale, well told. And, perhaps, to the enduring appeal of slightly sticky shortbread. The adventure, he thought, was truly just beginning. A new chapter awaited. And who knew what fantastical creatures it might bring to light?

A New Chapter

The flurry of interviews subsided, leaving Lachlan with a quiet contentment and a significantly larger research grant. His life, once a predictable cycle of lectures, lab work, and the occasional kiwi-spotting expedition, was now a kaleidoscope of unexpected colours. He'd traded his tweed jacket for a slightly more rugged, adventure-ready version, and his sensible brown shoes were replaced with sturdy hiking boots, worn and mud-splattered, testament to his recent exploits.

The phone call came on a blustery Tuesday afternoon, a jarring contrast to the quiet hum of his newly renovated lab. It was Professor Anya Sharma, a renowned ornithologist from the University of Auckland, her voice a vibrant counterpoint to the grey sky outside. "Lachlan, my dear fellow," she chirped, "I need your expertise. A most peculiar situation has arisen on the Chatham Islands."

The Chatham Islands. A remote archipelago, a thousand miles east of New Zealand, known for its unique flora and fauna, and notoriously difficult to reach. Lachlan's adventurous spirit stirred. The Haggis saga had opened a door to a world he hadn't known existed, a world where the improbable was not only possible, but commonplace.

"Apparently," Professor Sharma continued, "we have a...discrepancy. Our latest census of the Chatham Island Taiko, a flightless bird unique to these islands, shows a significant population drop. But there's no sign of predation, no disease outbreak, no obvious cause. We're stumped."

Lachlan, his curiosity piqued, was already mentally packing his bags. The Chatham Islands were a paradise for a zoologist – a pristine ecosystem teeming with unusual species, many found nowhere else on Earth. The mystery of the vanishing Taiko added an irresistible layer of intrigue.

Within days, Lachlan found himself on a small,

rickety plane, bouncing precariously above the turbulent ocean. Below, the islands emerged from the vast expanse of water, emerald green patches of land fringed by rugged coastlines. It felt like stepping back in time, a world untouched by the hurried pace of modern life.

His first few days were spent acclimating to the island's rhythm, a slower, more deliberate pace than he was accustomed to. He spent hours observing the local wildlife: the shy Chatham Island petrel, its call a mournful whisper in the night; the cheeky Chatham Island robin, unafraid of human proximity; and the enigmatic Chatham Island forget-me-not, its delicate blue flowers a splash of colour against the verdant landscape.

The Taiko, however, remained elusive. He spent days trekking through dense forests, traversing muddy swamps, and clambering over rocky cliffs, always searching for a sign of the flightless bird. He spoke with the local Moriori people, the island's indigenous inhabitants, who shared their knowledge of the land and its creatures, their stories weaving a rich tapestry of history and folklore.

Their accounts, though offering no concrete explanation for the Taiko's disappearance, were rich with local legends and ancient stories, some mentioning a mythical creature, a giant bird said to inhabit the heart of the island's largest forest, the 'Te Whanga'. This mythical beast, a guardian of the forest, was said to possess the power to shift the balance of nature, a powerful symbol in the Moriori culture.

Lachlan ventured into the Te Whanga, a dense, almost primeval forest, a labyrinth of towering trees and tangled undergrowth. The air was heavy with the scent of damp earth and decaying leaves, the silence punctuated only by the chirping of insects and the distant cry of a seabird. It felt as though the forest held its breath, anticipating his arrival.

Days bled into nights as Lachlan delved deeper into the mystery. He encountered strange phenomena: shimmering lights in the twilight, unsettling sounds echoing through the trees, and inexplicable shifts in the vegetation. He even found traces of unusual footprints, far too large for any known creature. Could the legendary guardian bird be real? The thought sent a thrilling shiver down his spine.

One evening, as a luminous mist swirled around him, he stumbled upon a hidden clearing. In the centre stood a magnificent tree, its branches draped with luminous moss, emitting a soft, ethereal glow. And beneath the tree, nestled amongst the roots, were a group of Taiko – not just a few, but a whole flock, far more numerous than anyone had anticipated.

But they weren't alone. Perched atop the ancient tree, its plumage shimmering with iridescent colours, sat a creature far exceeding the scope of any scientific understanding. It was magnificent, a feathered behemoth, its size dwarfing even the largest eagle, its eyes glowing with an otherworldly intelligence. This was the guardian bird of legend, magnificent and terrifying all at once.

Lachlan surmised that the avian protector, far from decimating the Taiko, was their vigilant guardian. With cunning precision, it had relocated the Taiko to an undisclosed sanctuary, a secluded refuge shielding them from the calamitous force that had precipitated their dwindling numbers. This act underscored the profound complexity of the ecosystem, where even the most extraordinary beings contribute to the delicate equilibrium of nature's grand design..

The discovery solved the mystery of the vanishing Taiko. It was not extinction, but relocation, orchestrated by a mythical creature that had previously existed only in legend. Lachlan documented his findings meticulously, carefully noting the behaviour of the Taiko and the guardian bird. He realised the importance of preserving the unique ecology of the Chatham Islands, protecting not only the known species but the mysterious and wondrous ones, too. The experience was transformative, solidifying his belief in the unexpected wonders of the natural world, a world where reality exceeded even the wildest flights of fancy.

His return to New Zealand was met with excitement and disbelief, as he unveiled his incredible discoveries. His tale, even more fantastical than his Haggis adventure, captivated the world, prompting a global initiative for the preservation of the Chatham Islands' ecosystem. His research led to new policies, stricter conservation measures, and a heightened awareness of the balance of nature. The world, he realised, was filled with extraordinary wonders, awaiting those willing to venture beyond the realm of the ordinary. And he, Lachlan McGregor, was ready for the next chapter. The world, it seemed, was a never-ending tapestry of wonder, waiting to be explored, one extraordinary creature at a time. He smiled. The next adventure was already calling, a whisper carried on the wind from a distant land, promising even more bizarre and beautiful encounters with nature's most surprising creations. The journey, he knew, was far from over.

Acknowledgments

First and foremost, a hearty "Sláinte!" to the resilient and remarkably tight-lipped inhabitants of the Isle of Skye. Your cryptic clues, dubious hospitality (that suspiciously peaty dram, Angus!), and general air of mystery made this

adventure truly unforgettable. Special thanks to Hamish, the shepherd with a surprisingly accurate knowledge of Haggis migratory patterns, and to Morag, whose shortbread fueled my research (and my questionable navigational skills).

My deepest gratitude also goes to my long-suffering agent, Penelope Featherstonehaugh, who patiently endured my increasingly frantic emails filled with blurry photographs of heather and questionable pronouncements about the

taxonomy of fictional creatures. Your unwavering belief in this project (despite my questionable sanity) is appreciated more than words can say.

Finally, a huge thank you to my editor, Barnaby "Barnacle Butt" Butterfield, whose meticulous editing kept this manuscript from veering too far into the realms of utter nonsense (though I suspect he secretly approves of my slightly unorthodox approach to zoological research).

Glossary

Haggis:

A legendary, possibly mythical, creature of the Scottish Highlands. Descriptions vary widely, ranging from a fluffy, six-legged beast to a rather grumpy, short-legged quadruped with a penchant for shortbread.

Sláinte:

Gaelic toast, roughly translating to "Cheers!" or "To your health!" Best enjoyed with a dram of something peaty. Drams:

A small measure of whisky, traditionally served in a thimble (or, occasionally, a chipped teacup).

Tweed:

A durable, woven fabric, traditionally associated with Scotland. Highly recommended for wear in the

unpredictable Scottish climate. Especially important when on the trail of an elusive Haggis.

References

Scottish Folklore for the Perplexed – Professor Alistair McTavish (1987) – A surprisingly helpful (if somewhat dry) guide to Scottish mythology.

The Complete Guide to Scottish Wildlife (Mostly) –

Professor Agnes McDougall (2001) – Less helpful on the Haggis front, but excellent for identifying other Highlands fauna.

Various pub conversations overheard on the Isle of Skye (2023) - Highly unreliable, but amusing nonetheless.

Author Biography

Lachlan McGregor (PhD, Zoology, University of Otago) is a world-renowned zoologist with a passion for obscure creatures, questionable scientific methods, and copious amounts of tweed. While his research into the Haggis remains highly controversial, he remains unconvinced that it was merely a hallucination induced by excessive whisky consumption. He currently resides in New Zealand, surrounded by a collection of taxidermied kiwi (mostly). When not chasing elusive creatures, Lachlan enjoys knitting, competitive sheep-shearing, and arguing vehemently about the merits of single-malt scotch. He is currently working on a new book, tentatively titled

The Curious Case of the

Singing Kelpies

.